PASSAGES™

MANUSCRIPT

3

ANNISON'S RISK

PAUL MCCUSKER

FROM ADVENTURES IN ODYSSEY®

TYNDALE
Tyndale House Publishers, Inc.
Wheaton, Illinois

ANNISON'S RISK
Copyright © 2005 by Focus on the Family.
All rights reserved. International copyright secured.

ISBN: 1-58997-169-8

Library of Congress has cataloged previous edition as follows:
McCusker, Paul. 1958-
    Annison's risk / by Paul McCusker.
        p. cm.
    Summary: Maddy slips into an alternate world called Marus where
she helps Queen Annison protect the believers in the Unseen One from
persecution.
    ISBN: 1-56179-809-6
    [1. Space and time Fiction. 2. Kings, queens, rulers, etc. Fiction.
3. Christian life Fiction.] I. Title.
    PZ7.M47841635An   1999
    [Fic]—dc21   99-36357
                                                              CIP

A Focus on the Family book published by
Tyndale House Publishers, Wheaton, Illinois 60189

TYNDALE is a registered trademark of Tyndale House Publishers, Inc.
Tyndale's quill logo is a trademark of Tyndale House Publishers, Inc.

The author is represented by the literary agency of Alive Communications,
7680 Goddard Street, Suite 200, Colorado Springs, CO 80920.

Editors: Larry Weeden and Mick Silva
Cover design: Greg Sills
Cover copy: Larrilee Frazier

Printed in the United States of America
2 3 4 5 6 7 8 9 /10 09 08 07 06 05

Adventures in Odyssey Presents
Passages, Book III

PROLOGUE

"It looks like we've reached a dead end," Jack Allen said to his friend John Avery Whittaker, or Whit, as he was better known. The two men were having lunch at Hal's Diner after spending the entire morning searching through archives at Odyssey City Hall and the Odyssey Public Library. They had been trying to solve a mystery

Whit chomped on a French fry, then thoughtfully brushed the side of his finger along his bushy, white mustache. His eyes scanned the papers, photocopies, and notes on the red Formica table in front of him. Around the diner, cups rattled, cutlery chinked, and people chatted. Cold sunlight, reflecting off the snow outside, poured in through the large, plate-glass windows. Whit sighed and said, "Maybe we missed something. Let's go over it again."

Jack nodded. He knew they would probably have to go over the "clues" repeatedly.

The mystery began when Jack discovered a school notebook in the bottom of a trunk that had belonged to an elderly schoolteacher named Maude McCutcheon. Maude had recently died, and her children had sold many of her belongings to Jack because he owned an antique shop. The notebook was

the old-fashioned kind: black with a white subject box on the
front, and black adhesive tape down the binding. Every page
was filled with handwriting that told a story about a brother
and sister named Kyle and Anna who visited their grandparents in the summer of 1958.

Being in a small town made the children bored and restless.
So, on the advice of an uncle, they took a walk through some
woods to a mysterious old house. Strange things began to happen while they searched the house, and suddenly they found
they were no longer in Odyssey. They had traveled to a country
called Marus—in another world—where they seemed to have
remarkable powers because of a being called the *Unseen One*.

Jack had been so intrigued by the story that he had shown
it to Whit. Whit had thought it fascinating and sensed immediately that there was more to it than just a class assignment or
fanciful imagination. They had then searched through the notebook to see if they could learn who wrote the tale. Apart from
the story itself, there were no clues.

Whit and Jack had wondered if Maude McCutcheon had any
other stories like it. So the next day—yesterday, in fact—they had
gone to the schoolteacher's house. Her son, who had never seen
the notebook before and didn't recognize the handwriting, had
invited them to have a look around. They had found a second
notebook on a shelf in Maude McCutcheon's study. Shoved
inside were newspaper clippings from August 1945 about the

United States dropping atomic bombs on Japan. The story inside was written in the same handwriting as the first. This one, though, told the story of a boy named Wade Mullens who, while waiting for his father to come home from World War II, slipped into Marus and accidentally brought a holocaust with him.

Whit and Jack had been even more intrigued after reading the second manuscript. It seemed to weave real-life events from Odyssey into the fantasy world of Marus. Who had written these stories, and why? The two men wanted to know.

And so Whit and Jack had spent the morning looking through archives at City Hall and newspapers at the library, try-ing to learn about Kyle and Anna and Wade Mullens. Now, in Hal's Diner, they sorted through the notebooks and papers and pages of scribble pads for clues—just like a couple of old pan-handlers sifting for gold.

"Let's start with what we know," Whit said. "The first note-book told the story of Kyle and Anna and how they helped Darien become king of Marus. But the story didn't tell us their last names, only that they were visiting their grandparents in the summer of 1958."

"That's right," Jack agreed. "The adventure happened that summer, but the notebook was written on October 3, 1958."

Whit pushed some papers aside and glanced at the notes he'd written. "In the second manuscript, we read the story of Wade Mullens. Wade's mother was Carol, and his father was Ronald."

Jack looked at his own notes. "We know that Ronald had been hurt and trapped on an island in the South Pacific when the war ended, but he was found and brought back to Odyssey. Then ..." Jack held up a yellow newspaper clipping "... in the article reporting Ronald's return, Wade said he was thankful to the 'Unseen One' for bringing his father back. Wade said the Unseen One was God."

"Funny that he'd mention it. The Unseen One must've seemed very real to him." Whit gazed out the window, squinting against the bright sunlight. Cars drove past, sending up plumes of melting snow from the road.

Jack continued reading from his notes. "Wade went to the usual schools here in Odyssey Maude McCutcheon was his English teacher in eighth grade."

"So that's our first real connection." Whit drew a line connecting Wade's name with Maude McCutcheon's on his notepad.

"Later, Wade followed in his father's footsteps and joined the military. He became a pilot for the Air Force in 1956." Jack picked up another article that had a black-and-white picture of Wade as a decorated officer. "In 1965, it was reported that Wade had been killed in Vietnam."

Whit stroked his chin. He'd lost a son in Vietnam, too, and could imagine how Ronald and Carol Mullens felt. "If the old phone directories are anything to go by, the Mullens family lived in Odyssey at least until 1966. City Hall records show that they sold their house in February of that year. We don't know where they moved to."

Jack leaned back in his chair and folded his hands across his chest. He felt he had nearly gone cross-eyed searching through databases and the Internet to find where the Mullenses might be now. Nothing matched up. "So we've reached a dead end," he said.

Whit shook his head. "There must be some other angle, another avenue, we can consider."

"Like what?"

"We could talk to their old neighbors. Somebody's bound to know where they went."

"And how will we explain our questions to the neighbors?"

"What do you mean?"

Jack pretended to be standing in front of one of the neighbors' doors. "Hello there, we're trying to track down the Mullens family because their son Wade was in a story about traveling to another world."

Whit laughed at the thought.

"They'll think we're crazy" Jack smiled. "We *are* crazy. Imagine spending all this time trying to find the author of a couple of kids' stories."

"Do you really think they're only kids' stories?"

Whit's question was so earnest that Jack paused to think

about it for a moment. *Something* about the stories made them both wonder if maybe, just *maybe,* the stories really happened. It was crazy, sure. But *what if?*

Maggie, their waitress, approached with a coffeepot and held it up with a smile.

"Yes, please," Jack said. She poured the steaming drink into his mug.

"Whit?"

Whit nudged his mug in her direction. "Thank you, Maggie."

After Maggie poured his coffee, she gestured to the papers and asked, "Aren't you two a little old to be doing homework?"

"Old?" Jack asked innocently and looked to Whit. "What's she talking about? Who's old?"

"We're playing detectives," Whit said.

"Oh, really?"

Whit eyed her as if he suddenly realized something. "Maggie, you grew up here in Odyssey, didn't you?"

"Born in Connellsville, raised in Odyssey," she replied.

"How old are you?"

"That's none of your business."

"I mean, when did you go to school? The late forties? Early fifties?"

"Yes to both decades. I graduated from high school in 1953."

"Did you know Wade Mullens?"

Maggie looked surprised and set the coffeepot down on the table. "Wade? Yeah, I knew Wade. We had some classes together. I even had a crush on him once. Why do you ask?"

Whit and Jack exchanged hopeful glances.

"Do you have any idea what became of his parents after Wade died in Vietnam?" Whit asked.

"They moved away."

"Do you know where?"

"They moved to Virginia. Wade's father got a job there. They wanted to get out of Odyssey because it reminded them so much of Wade."

"You say that as if you know firsthand," Jack observed. "Were you friends with the Mullenses?"

"Mrs. Mullens and I became friends because of Wade."

Whit shifted in his seat excitedly. "Have you kept in touch? Do you know where they are now?"

"Well, Mr. Mullens died nearly 10 years ago, and Mrs. Mullens remarried. Her name is Walston now."

"Where's she living?" Jack asked.

Maggie suddenly frowned. "What's this all about? Why are you so interested in finding her?"

"We want to ask her a couple of questions about these notebooks," Whit said, waving a hand over them.

"What about them?"

"They have stories in them. One is about Wade."

Maggie was puzzled. "A story about Wade? What kind of story?"

"A story about a place called Marus," Jack said.

Maggie's features froze in place, as if she had been stunned.

Whit pressed on. "Did you ever hear Wade talk about a place called Marus?"

Maggie's face changed, as if she wanted to appear cool and relaxed, but she still replied quickly and nervously. "Marus? Why should I? Look, I have to take care of these other tables." She grabbed the coffeepot and hurried away.

"But Maggie," Whit called out after her, "where is Mrs. Mullens?"

Maggie said over her shoulder, "Mrs. *Walston* lives in Connellsville. On Meadowbrook Lane."

Carol Walston lived in a small, gray, boxlike house with shutters on the windows and a white picket fence. A man who turned out to be George Walston, Carol's husband, was scraping the last of the snow off his driveway when Whit and Jack drove up. He stopped shoveling long enough to rub his red-checkered coat sleeve across his sweaty forehead. The movement knocked his wool cap slightly askew. A tuft of white hair poked out. "What can I do for you gents?" he asked.

"We're looking for Carol Walston," Whit answered.

"Are you salesmen?" he asked, hooking a thumb at the briefcase Whit carried at his side.

"Not at all," Jack replied. "We're from Odyssey. We want to talk to her about her son."

"Oh." George Walston turned away as if mentioning Carol's son was a cue not to get involved. "She's inside. Just knock hard on the front door."

"Thank you," Whit said. But George was already pushing the snow shovel across the driveway again.

Carol Walston was a surprisingly tall, slender woman with a round, friendly face. It was hard to guess her age since her face seemed almost wrinkle-free and her hair was dyed a flaming red. She wiped her hands on her apron and invited Whit and Jack inside.

"So what's this all about?" she asked after she'd taken their coats and got them seated comfortably in the living room.

Whit explained about finding the two manuscripts and the trail that had led them to her. He also pulled out of his briefcase the two school notebooks and the articles that had been tucked inside. Whit thought he saw something in her eyes—a glint of great interest in the notebooks—but she seemed to restrain herself and laughed instead.

"Wade would laugh, too," she said. "He would. To think of two grown men making such a fuss about his little story."

"You remember it?" Jack asked.

"Of course I do," Mrs. Walston said. "He came out of that fever—the flu was going around then—and told me all about the dream he'd had."

"Is this Wade's handwriting?" Whit asked, holding out one of the notebooks.

"No," she replied without looking at the book. "But Wade was a very imaginative boy. Very intelligent. He must've told his story to some of his friends, and I can only guess that one of them wrote it down for a school assignment." Her gaze drifted to a black-and-white photo sitting in a gold frame on the end table. A young man posed proudly in a military uniform.

Whit asked, "Did he ever talk to you about Marus after that?"

"He mentioned it occasionally. But only the way a child mentions a game he once loved to play I didn't pay much attention."

"So he didn't tell any more stories—or write any down anywhere?"

Mrs. Walston shook her head. "Not that I know of."

Jack held up the other notebook. "Then how did this *other* story, written 12 years later, come about?"

Mrs. Walston shrugged. "I couldn't tell you."

Whit and Jack looked at each other sadly.

Mrs. Walston smiled at them. "I'm sorry for you both, but you really shouldn't take children's stories so seriously." She stood up and began to smooth her apron. "If you two will excuse me, I really have to get back to my baking. My great-nephews birthday is next Saturday, and I promised to bake him a Texas sheet cake."

With nothing else to say, Whit and Jack put on their coats and made their way to the front door. A door slammed in another part of the house, and Mr. Walston appeared at the kitchen doorway. His cap was off now, his thin, white hair matted to his head.

"Did you wipe your feet?" Mrs. Walston asked him.

"Sure did," Mr. Walston answered and held up a boot to prove it. "Are you leaving so soon?" he asked Jack and Whit.

"Yes. It was nice to meet you," Jack said.

Just as he and Whit were about to step out into the cold day, Whit turned back to Mrs. Walston. To Jack's surprise, he asked, "Do you believe Marus really exists?"

Mrs. Walston laughed sharply "No," she replied. "Why would I? Wade had a vivid imagination, he was feverish, and we were both worried about his father's safe return from the South Pacific."

"I see."

"Thank you for coming by, though," she said as they stepped onto the front stoop. "It was a sweet reminder of my son."

"Marus?" Mr. Walston said from the kitchen. "Did you say Marus?"

Annoyed, Mrs. Walston snapped, "Mind your own business, George."

He ignored her and moved into the hallway from the kitchen. "I remember reading that story. The one by Wade, right?"

Mr. Walston shrugged. "Didn't he?"

"You're confused, George," Mrs. Walston said.

Whit and Jack glanced at each other.

"You read Wade's story? When he went to Marus?" Jack asked.

"Must've been a long time ago," Mrs. Walston said quickly.

Mr. Walston now looked puzzled. "When *Wade* went to Marus? No. I read a story he wrote about a girl named—oh, I don't remember—anyway, some other kid went to Marus."

"Kyle and Anna?" Whit persisted.

"Not two kids. Just one."

Then there's another notebook, Whit and Jack seemed to say to each other in their expressions. The color left Mrs. Walston's cheeks.

Whit opened his briefcase, grabbed the notebooks, and asked, "Was it written in a notebook? Like these?"

Mr. Walston smiled. "Yep. Just the same." Then he looked perplexed. "You have two of them already I didn't know there was more than the one."

Mrs. Walston looked as if she wanted to throttle her husband. "Drop it, George," she said in a threatening tone. She tried to move Whit and Jack toward the door. "Thanks again for coming—"

"Mrs. Walston, if you have another notebook, we'd be grateful to see it," Whit said.

She stammered for a moment, then said, "I don't have it. My husband is old and easily confused. If there's a notebook, it'll be in the attic with my son's schoolbooks."

Mr. Walston grunted and replied, "That's ridiculous, Carol! It's in the TV room. I saw it there just the other day." He suddenly disappeared from view. His footsteps thudded down another hallway. In the meantime, Mrs. Walston regained the color in her cheeks. They now went a bright red as Mr. Walston returned with an old-fashioned school notebook in his hand.

"See?" he said proudly. "It's right here."

"So it is," Mrs. Walston said softly.

"May we see it?" Jack asked. Mr. Walston handed the notebook over to him. At a glance, it was obvious to both Jack and Whit that the handwriting was the same as in the other two. But the story was different.

"Mrs. Walston, it would mean a lot to us if we could borrow this to read," said Whit.

"It's a keepsake," she replied in a sharp tone. "I'd rather not let it go."

"Then please come with us while we make copies of it."

"No," she insisted. "It's my son's story, and I don't want it out in public."

Whit smiled and said gently, "But it can't be your son's story. You already told us it wasn't his handwriting."

Mr. Walston looked befuddled. "What's the matter with you, Carol?" he asked. "If they want to read the story, let them."

It was clear that Mrs. Walston had run out of sensible reasons to keep Whit and Jack from having the notebook. A slight groan escaped from her before she said, "All right, I'll trust you with it. But only for the night. And *no copies.*"

"If you insist," Whit said.

They took the notebook, thanked her, and walked out.

The door slammed behind them, and they heard Mrs. Walston shout unhappily, "George!"

This was followed by Mr. Walston complaining, "What? What did I do wrong?"

During the ride back to Odyssey, Whit said to Jack, "I thought something odd was going on."

"You did? Why?"

"When I took the notebooks out of my briefcase, I thought I saw something in her eyes. As if she already knew what they were. But more than that, it struck me as odd that she didn't ask to read the stories. She didn't even look at them."

"So?"

"If someone brought a story to you about your dead son, wouldn't you want to read it?"

"Well ... I suppose I would," Jack said. The whole experience was bizarre, he thought. "So what do you think she's hiding? Why didn't she want us to see this manuscript?"

Whit gazed down at the notebook in his lap. "I have no idea. Maybe we'll understand more after we read it."

"You'd better start now if we hope to finish it tonight."

Whit opened the cover, his eye drawn to the familiar handwriting.

It was dated September 18, 1927.

"The Chronicles of Intercession," it said.

And then the story began.

❖————————❖

"Ready or not, here I come!" a child's voice called out from somewhere behind the shed.

Madina Nicholaivitch giggled and scrambled to find a hiding place. She'd already hidden once behind the well and once in the garage, and now she had to think of somewhere little Johnny Ziegler wouldn't think to find her.

Johnny shouted, excitement in his voice, "I'm coming, Maddy!"

Everyone called her Maddy now except her grandparents, who still spoke in Russian and called her Dreamy Madina in that tongue. It didn't matter to them that they'd been living in America, this town of Odyssey, for 10 years now. "We will not forsake our traditions, no matter where we live," Grandma had said.

On the other hand, Maddy's father, Boris, now refused to speak any Russian. He said he was protesting the Russian Revolution of 1917 that drove them, persecuted and destitute, from their home in St. Petersburg. "We're in America now," he stated again and again in his clipped English. "We must speak as Americans."

"The revolution will not last," Maddy's Grandpa proclaimed several times a year, especially in October, on the anniversary of the revolution.

"It is now 1927, is it not?" Maddy's father argued. "They have killed the czar, they have destroyed everything we once held dear, and they are closing our churches. I turn my back on Russia as Russia turned its back on us. We are Americans now."

So Madina became Maddy and spoke American because she was only two when they came to America. She never really learned Russian anyway, except for odd phrases from her grandparents. Refugees that they were, they'd started off in New York and drifted west to Chicago as opportunities from various friends and relatives presented themselves. Boris had been an accomplished tailor back in St. Petersburg, so his skill was in demand wherever they went. Then they'd heard from a cousin who owned a tailor shop in the small town of Odyssey and wanted Boris to join him in the business. They called the firm Nichols Tailor & Clothes, Nichols being the English corruption of their original Russian name, and made clothes for nearly everyone, including the mayor of Odyssey.

Maddy was unaffected by all the changes and upheaval in their lives. She seemed contented and happy regardless of where they were. The world could have been falling apart around her and she would have carried on in her pleasant, dreamlike way, lost in fantasies like *Alice in Wonderland, Peter Pan,* and the many other stories she read at the local library.

She often pretended to be a girl with magical powers in a fairy-tale world. Or she played out a dream she'd been having night after night for the past two weeks. In the dream, she was a lady-in-waiting to a princess with raven black hair and the most beautiful face Maddy had ever seen.

"You must come and help me," the princess said to her every night in the dream.

"I will," Maddy replied. And then she would wake up.

She had told her mother about the dream. But her mother smiled indulgently and dismissed it as she had most of Maddy's fanciful ideas.

Apart from pretending to be in fairy tales, Maddy enjoyed playing games like hide-and-seek with the smaller neighborhood children. Her mother often said that she would be a teacher when she grew up because she loved books and children so much.

Maddy circled their old farm-style house that had been built with several other similar houses on the edge of town. It had gray shingles, off-white shutters, and a long porch along the front. She ducked under the clothesline that stretched from the porch post to a nearby pole. The shirts and underclothes brushed comfortingly against her face, warmed by the sun. She then spied a small break in the trelliswork that encased the underside of the porch. That would be her hiding place, she decided—under the porch.

She pressed a hand down on her thick, curly, brown hair to keep it from getting caught on any of the trellis splinters and went only as far under as she dared, to the edge of the shadows. The dirt under her hands and bare legs was cold. She tried not to get any of it on her dark blue peasant dress, which her father had made especially for her. She could smell the damp earth and old wood from the porch. In another part of the garden, she heard her little brother squeal with delight as their mother played with him in the late-summer warmth.

"I'm going to find you," little Johnny, the boy from next door, called out.

Maddy held her breath as she saw his legs appear through the diamond shapes of the trellis. He hesitated, but the position of his feet told her that he had his back to the porch. Maybe he wouldn't see the gap she'd crawled through. He moved farther along, getting closer to the gap, so she moved farther back into the shadows and darkness. The hair on her neck bristled. She'd always worried that a wild animal might have gone under the porch to live, just as their dog Babushka had when she'd given birth to seven puppies last year. But

Maddy's desire to keep Johnny from finding her was greater than her fear, so she went farther back and farther in.

The porch, like a large mouth, seemed to swallow her in darkness. The trelliswork, the sunlight, and even Johnny's legs, now moving to and fro along the porch, faded away as if she'd slowly closed her eyes. But she knew she hadn't. She held her hand up in front of her face and wiggled her fingers. She could see still them.

Then, from somewhere behind her, a light grew, like the rising of a sun. But it wasn't yellow like dawn sunlight; it was white and bright, like the sun at noon. She turned to see, wondering where the light had come from. She knew well that there couldn't be a light farther under the porch, that she would soon reach a dead end at the cement wall of the basement.

As she looked at the light, she began to hear noises as well. At first they were indistinct, but then she recognized them as the sounds of people talking and moving. Maddy wondered if friends from town had come to visit. But the voices were too numerous for a small group of friends. This sounded more like a big crowd. And mixed with the voices were the distinct sounds of horses whinnying and the clip-clop of their hooves and the grating of wagon wheels on a stony street.

Crawling crablike and being careful not to bump her head on the underside of the porch, Maddy moved in the direction of the light and sounds. The noises grew louder, and, once she squinted a little, she could see human and horse legs moving back and forth, plus the distinct outline of wagon wheels.

It's a busy street, she thought, but then she reminded herself, *There's no busy street near our house*. The sight inflamed her imagination, and she ventured still closer and closer to the scene. *It's like crawling out of a small cave*, she thought. Then her mind raced to the many stories she'd read about children who had stepped through a hole or mirror or doorway and wound up in a magical land. Her heart beat excitedly as she thought—*hoped*—that maybe it was about to happen to her. Perhaps she would get to see something wondrous; perhaps she was going to enter a fairy tale.

At the edge of the darkness, she glanced up and realized she was no longer under the porch. The coarse planks of plywood and the two wheels directly in front of her and two wheels directly behind her made her think she must be under a wagon. More startling was that the porch, the trellis, Johnny, and even her house had disappeared.

A man shouted, "Yah!" and snapped leather reins, and the wagon moved away from her. She stayed still, afraid she might get caught under the wheels, but they didn't touch her. In a moment she was crouched in an open space, sunlight pouring down onto her. People were crowded around, and she stood up with embarrassment on her face, certain they were wondering who she was and where she'd come from.

A man grabbed her arm and pulled her quickly into the crowd. "You'd better get out of the road, little lady," he warned. "Do you want to get run over by the procession?"

Besides that, no one seemed to notice her. But she noticed them. Her eyes were dazzled by the bright colors of the hundreds—maybe even thousands—of people lined up on both sides of the avenue. Trees sprung out from among them like green fountains. Tall buildings stood behind them with enormous columns and grand archways. Maddy blinked again. The colors seemed too bright somehow, much richer than the colors she was used to seeing. Then she smiled to herself: They looked just like the colors in so many of the illustrated stories she'd read.

She noticed that some of the people clutched flags and

banners, while others held odd-looking, rectangular-shaped hats to their chests, and a few carried children up on their shoulders. What struck Maddy most were the peculiar garments everyone wore. The women were in long, frilly dresses, not unlike Maddy's own peasant dress but far more intricate in their design, billowing out at the waist like tents. The men had on long coats and trousers that only went to just below their knees. The rest of their legs were covered with white stockings. On their feet they wore leather shoes with large, square buckles. The men had ponytails, she noticed, and hats that came to three-pointed corners.

The scene reminded her of the last Fourth of July, when she had stood along Main Street with the rest of Odyssey for the big parade, followed by fireworks and picnic food in the park. Some of the people in that parade had dressed the same as the people she saw now. It was the style of clothes worn when America won its independence.

Unlike the parade in Odyssey, however, this parade didn't seem very happy. Most of the people stood with stern expressions on their faces. A few looked grieved. Several women wiped tears from their eyes. Maddy suspected she had formed the wrong impression of what she was seeing. Maybe it wasn't a parade; maybe it was a funeral procession.

"Did someone die?" Maddy asked the man who'd pulled her from the street.

He gazed at her thoughtfully and replied, "Our nation, little lady Our nation."

A regiment of soldiers now marched down the avenue. The men were dressed in the same outfits as those in the crowd, but all were a solid blue color, and they had helmets on their heads and spears or swords in their hands. They broke their ranks and spread out to the edge of the crowd.

"The king is coming, and we want you to be excited about it," one of them said gruffly.

"He's not *our* king!" someone shouted from the thick of the crowd.

The soldier held up his sword menacingly. "You can be excited or arrested," he threatened. "The choice is yours."

The soldiers moved off to stir up other parts of the crowd. Across the avenue, a fight broke out, and Maddy watched in horror as three soldiers began to beat and kick a man they'd knocked down. They dragged him away while the rest of the soldiers stood with their swords and spears at the ready.

What kind of parade is this, she wondered, *where the people are forced to enjoy it or be beaten?* As if to answer her question, Maddy remembered the stories her father told of the Russian revolutionaries who demanded that people parade and salute even when they didn't want to.

Halfhearted cheers worked their way through the crowd as a parade of horses approached and passed, soldiers sitting erect on their backs, swords held high in a formal salute. Then a large band of musicians with woodwinds and brass instruments came by, playing a lively song of celebration. Next came several black, open-topped carriages, each with people dressed in colorful outfits of gold and silver that twinkled in the sunlight. The men wore white shirts with lacy collars. The women wore hats with brightly colored feathers sticking out of the backs. They waved and smiled at the crowd.

Maddy noticed one man in particular who seemed almost as unhappy as some of the people in the crowd. He had a pockmarked face, unfriendly eyes, a narrow nose, and thinning, wiry hair. Unlike the rest of the parade, he didn't wear a colorful jacket but one of solid black—as if he, too, were mourning something. Occasionally he lifted his hand in a wave, but

Maddy was struck by the look of boredom on his face. It seemed to require considerable effort for him to be pleasant to the crowd.

At the end of this particular procession came the largest carriage of all. Gold on the outside, its seats were made of a plush, red material. A man sat alone on the rear seat—propped up somehow to raise him higher than he normally would have been—and waved happily at the crowds. He was a pleasant-looking, middle-aged man with ruddy cheeks, big eyes, and wild, curly hair.

"I was wondering if he'd wear that stupid wig," someone muttered nearby.

"It's no worse than that coat," someone else commented.

The man's coat displayed the colors of the rainbow and had large buttons on the front. Maddy smiled. It made him look a little like a clown.

"I can't bear it," a woman cried as large tears streamed down her face. Even with the tears, she waved a small flag back and forth.

"What's wrong?" Maddy asked the woman. "Why are you crying?"

The woman dabbed at her face with a handkerchief. "Because it's the end of us all," she replied with a sniffle.

"Aye," an elderly man behind her agreed. "When the barbarians parade down the streets of Sarum, it's the end of Marus."

Suddenly a group of soldiers who had been following the golden carriage with muskets slung over their shoulders spread out to the crowds, thrusting flags and banners into their hands. "Take these and follow us to the palace," they commanded.

"Only after I've had my brain replaced with a beetroot," the elderly man said defiantly.

A soldier hit him in the stomach with the butt of his musket. The man doubled over in pain. "You'll follow no matter what kind of brain you have!" the soldier growled.

"Leave us alone!" a woman shouted. "Why don't you go back to Palatia where you belong?"

"And deprive our king of his spoils?" another soldier called back. "That wouldn't do."

The man who'd been hit recovered his breath, grumbled something Maddy didn't understand, then stepped out onto the avenue to follow the soldiers. Maddy was swept along with him and the rest of the crowd around her. Before she knew it, the man's flag—a small, rectangular cloth of red with a single star in the middle—was in her hand. He smiled at her. "You'll enjoy waving it more than I will," he suggested with a pained expression on his face. Eventually, she lost him in the crowd.

Worried that she might get in trouble, Maddy held the flag up and swung it as she walked. It didn't occur to her that she had no idea where she was or if she could find her way back to her porch. If this was a dream she was having or, better still, a magical place she'd found like Alice in Wonderland, she was curious to see what would happen next. "Dreamy Madina" was like that. But she wasn't too pleased about the nasty soldiers or the unhappiness of the people.

Maddy followed the crowd up the avenue until it joined yet another broad street. They seemed to walk for miles. Because she was surrounded on all sides by the crowd, she couldn't see much of the city. Only occasionally did a large building poke skyward beyond someone's head or shoulder. She wished she could stop to look longer at the great pillars and round towers or to read the names on the statues of men in brave and noble postures. Otherwise, she caught only glimpses of shops and homes made of brick and stone.

Just as Maddys legs started to ache from the long walk, the crowd slowed to a halt. Then, after a moment, it slowly moved forward again, now through a large gate made of wrought iron and gold posts. She found herself in a parklike area with level grounds and manicured grass. A single driveway curved around in a half-moon shape and stopped at the double front doors of a palace. At least Maddy assumed it was a palace, for she'd never seen such a majestic building in her life.

The front door stood at the center of two wings, made of yellow stone, that spread out to the left and the right. There were three stories, each with rows of tall windows that reflected the day like jewels. Maddy's eye was drawn to a gold rotunda over the center section, where the front doors were. On top of the rotunda was a statue of something that looked to her like an angel.

The crowd was instructed by the soldiers to sit down on the grass. The man in the golden carriage stood up to address the throng. His voice was deep and booming but still hard to hear since he was some distance away.

"I, King Willem, declare a national holiday for my subjects, the people of Marus," he declared.

"We're not your subjects!" a man shouted from somewhere deep in the crowd. Soldiers instantly moved in to find the culprit.

The king ignored him. "Let this be a time of celebration!" he continued. "A time of feasts and banquets unlike anything seen in your lifetime!"

"As if I ever expected to see a *Palatian* king on the throne in my lifetime," an old man with a craggy face growled softly off to Maddy's right.

"Let the musicians make music, let sweet drinks flow, and let the food fill our bellies!" the king called out. "From this day forward, Palatia *and* Marus are intertwined, united by fate and by victory."

"It's *our* fate thanks to *his* victory," the same man muttered sarcastically.

The king continued, "And now I beseech every man, woman, and child to join me in celebrating my marriage to one of your own, the pure and gracious Annison!"

With this, a woman stepped out through one of the palace's front doors. Maddy gasped. The woman had raven black hair and a slender face, with a smile that seemed to light up everything around her. It was the most beautiful face Maddy had ever seen.

"It's the princess from my dream," she said out loud to a woman next to her.

The woman grunted and turned away.

Maddy craned her neck to see better. Annison wore a beautiful, red-velvet dress that highlighted the redness of her lips and the blush of her cheeks. She looked shy and slightly embarrassed to be standing in front of so many people. Lifting her hand, she gave an awkward wave.

Though it was a slight gesture, the crowd came alive now, with all the people leaping to their feet to cheer her. They cheered in a way they hadn't cheered for the king at any point in his procession—wildly and exuberantly. He didn't seem to mind, though. He stretched out his hand to her, his face filled with pride.

"I can't believe she's marrying him," a woman nearby sneered in the midst of the shouts and cheers. "She's a Marutian. She should be ashamed."

"She's an orphan girl," another woman said with a shrug. "Who knows what her lineage is? For all we know, she's a Palatian herself."

"She may be our only hope," an old man observed thoughtfully. The two women looked at him uncomfortably and shut up.

Maddy didn't understand what any of it meant. All she knew was that the princess of her dream was real in this strange world, and now she'd lost sight of her because of the crowd.

"You must come and help me," the princess had said in the dream.

And Maddy had promised she would. With that thought in mind, she pressed herself forward through the crowd. She was determined to get to the front door of the palace—and Annison.

The king, who had resumed his speech while Maddy worked her way to the front of the audience, had just finished when she reached the edge of the lawn and the gravel driveway. The wheels of the golden carriage were within her reach. The king stepped down from the carriage, allowed Annison to put her arm through his, and walked with her into the palace. The large doors closed. Maddy was overcome with disappointment.

The soldiers began urging the crowd to disperse. Maddy stood alone where she was, her eyes fixed on the front doors, unsure of what to do next. She wanted—*needed*—to get to Annison. The feeling stabbed at her heart like a stitch. She didn't know why it was so important, yet the longing, the yearning, demanded that she make good on her promise to help Annison. But how could she get inside the palace?

The answer came from a stern-looking, matronly woman who suddenly appeared at her side. "You, child," she said.

Maddy looked up. "Me?" she asked.

"Didn't I see you with the choir?"

"Choir?"

"Stop answering my questions with questions. Are you with the choir or aren't you? If you are, you should be inside with the rest."

Maddy decided not to risk the wrath of this woman by asking what she was talking about. Besides, if joining the choir meant she might get to see Annison again, she was glad to join the choir. "How do I get in?" she inquired.

The woman grunted as if she had known all along that Maddy wasn't where she was supposed to be. "That way," she said and, taking Maddy's arm, led her to the double front doors.

A servant opened one of the doors before they reached it. He lifted a quizzical eyebrow.

"She's with the choir," the matronly woman explained.

He nodded and took Maddy's other arm, gently pulling her away from the matronly woman and into the front hall. It was an ornate foyer filled with paintings, statues, and a wide, marble staircase. The walls were trimmed with gold-leaf borders. A set of chandeliers hung like large diamonds on each side. Up above, Maddy saw that the inside of the rotunda contained frescoes of angels all around.

"I do wish you children would stay together," the servant said impatiently. He took Maddy down a grand hallway lined with more paintings and small alcoves with statues. Eventually they reached another double doorway. "They're preparing to rehearse here in the Great Hall," he said and nudged her inside.

Maddy's jaw dropped at the sight of the room. It truly was a great hall, with high walls of carved wood, cornices, ornately framed portraits, and mirrors. The tall windows she'd seen outside were ablaze with the daylight, which flooded the room. Dozens and dozens of tables were set up and being laid by more servants than Maddy could count. At one end of the hall was a small stage where a group of girls and boys stood, dressed in smart, gray outfits.

Maddy navigated her way past the tables and servants and approached the group cautiously. "Are you the choir?" she asked a girl with reddish hair who shifted uneasily from foot to foot.

"Yes," she replied. "We're going to sing for the king and his bride-to-be at the banquet tonight. My name is Sarah. Who are you?"

"My name is Maddy."

"You're not part of our choir," Sarah observed, then looked her over. "You're not in uniform."

"I know that."

"Then what are you doing here?"

"A woman outside told me to come in."

"To join us? Can you sing?"

"A little."

"I can sing, too." Sarah smiled. "I have a solo."

Maddy looked around, hoping to catch sight of Annison again. "Do you know where the princess—I mean, Annison—is?"

"She's probably in her chambers now," Sarah replied. "I think she's beautiful, don't you?"

"Yes, I do," Maddy said dreamily, then asked, "Do you know who she is?"

"She's Annison. You just said so."

"But *who* is she?"

The girl didn't seem to understand the question and shrugged.

Maddy decided to try a different approach. "I'm a stranger here—"

"Where are you from?"

"I come from Odyssey."

"Is that in Marus or Palatia?"

"It's in America."

Sarah looked puzzled, then shook her head. "I don't know where that is. But my father said that people were coming from all over the world for the wedding."

Maddy pressed on. "What I'm trying to say is that I'm a stranger and I don't know anything about this place or your king or—"

"Oh." Sarah lowered her head a little and said softly, "Well, for one thing, he's not really our king."

"He isn't?"

"No. He's not from Marus. He's from Palatia."

"So?"

Sarah looked at Maddy impatiently. "They beat us in a war and killed our old king—King Jarrod—and now Willem says *he's* our king, even though a lot of people here don't like him. My father says he's trying to turn Marus into Palatia."

"Then why don't the people throw him out?"

"We're not strong enough."

Maddy understood now. It was a little like Russia, where one side beat the other and took over everything. Something still didn't make sense, however. "But Annison is from Marus, isn't she?" she asked.

"Uh huh."

"Then why is she marrying the king?"

"Because he's the king and he said she has to," Sarah answered simply.

"Oh." Maddy suddenly felt sad that Annison was being forced to marry the king. That kind of story never had a happy ending in the fairy tales she'd read.

Sarah seemed to sense that more needed to be said and explained, "You see, the king was looking for someone to be his wife, and he made a command that all the prettiest girls in Sarum had to come to a big party he had here at the palace. Annison came, and she was the most beautiful girl he had ever seen, and so he asked her to marry him."

"Like Cinderella," Maddy said.

Sarah looked blankly at Maddy. "What?"

"Cinderella." Maddy was so relieved that she didn't notice Sarah's confused expression. "If this is like Cinderella, it might turn out all right."

"I don't know what you're talking about."

Maddy was still lost in her thoughts about the fairy tale. She asked, "Is Annison the daughter of a man who marries a terrible woman and has wicked stepsisters who make her work hard but won't let her come to the royal ball?"

Sarah pondered the question for a moment, her mind trying to sort out what Maddy had just asked. "Nobody really knows anything about Annison," she finally said, hoping it fit in somehow. "I heard she was an orphan who was raised in secret here in Sarum. My mother says she's probably the descendant of one of our ancient kings and would have been queen anyway even if King Willem hadn't conquered us. The king says she must be of royal lineage or she wouldn't be so beautiful. My father says it's just a move by the king to make the people of Marus like him better."

Maddy thought about it for a moment and concluded excitedly that maybe she was there to help Annison escape from the king, and then she could marry her true love, who was probably a handsome country lad who was really the son of a nobleman.

A thin, storklike woman walked in. Her hair was pulled back in a tight bun, and her dress hung on her skeletal frame like tissues wrapped around a coatrack. She clapped her hands. "Attention, children, attention!" she called.

All the children suddenly formed into two rows. Maddy tried to stay behind Sarah in the back.

"Is everyone here?" the woman asked.

"Yes, Mrs. Leichter," the children said in unison.

At the far end of the hall, a tall man entered. Maddy immediately remembered him from the parade. He was the one with a pockmarked complexion who looked bored and miserable. He made his way toward them. His hands were clasped behind his back, and he eyed them with the look of a vulture considering its next meal.

"Quickly," Mrs. Leichter said when she saw the man coming. "It's the king's personal assistant. Let's impress him with our singing by doing 'Fair Maiden.'"

The children stood up straight and waited for their cue to begin. Mrs. Leichter raised her arms and brought them down quickly. The children began to sing a lively tune about a fair maiden who was lost and lonely but met a handsome prince on a deserted road and won him over with her purity. Maddy stayed in the back, pretending to mouth the words. The tune was so catchy, though, that by the fifth verse she knew the words of the chorus and found herself singing along:

"Fair maiden, fair maiden," the prince said so sure,
"In all of my life there is no one so pure.
I'll take you as bride, I'll make you my queen
And rule o'er the land, and rule o'er the sea."

What Maddy didn't realize was that after the fifth verse, only the first half of the chorus was sung, with the rest of it hummed in harmony. So when the other children began to hum, she continued to sing loudly.

She realized her error right away but kept singing in hopes that it might not sound like a mistake. The other children began to giggle, however, and soon the song was completely undone.

Mrs. Leichter turned to the pockmarked man. "I'm so sorry, Lord Hector," she said in humiliation.

Hector grunted. "I hope it'll be improved before your performance tonight," he sneered and strode away.

Mrs. Leichter screwed up her eyes angrily and looked at Maddy. "Who are you, and what are you doing in my choir?" she demanded.

"I'm Maddy."

"But you don't belong in my choir."

"No, ma'am."

"Then I must ask you to step aside."

"But she can sing," Sarah said in her defense.

"I just heard her singing abilities," Mrs. Leichter said. "And while her voice is lovely, she obviously doesn't know the songs we're going to sing for the king and our future queen."

Maddy looked away sheepishly.

Mrs. Leichter flicked her hand at Maddy as if she were shooing a fly away. "Go on, my dear. If you wish to join our choir, have your parents come to the Academy and fill out the appropriate forms."

Maddy stepped away from the choir.

"Good-bye," Sarah said sadly.

"Good-bye." Maddy turned away, worried that Mrs. Leichter or one of the servants would now step forward and escort her from the palace. Any hope she had of meeting Annison seemed to vanish.

Mrs. Leichter turned her attention back to her choir and called out, "Attention, children. We will sing 'Fair Maiden' again, but correctly this time." She began to wave her hands, and the children started to sing as Maddy made her way across the Great Hall to the doors.

As she entered the long hallway again, it occurred to her that she had no idea of where to go. Worse, she realized she was being reckless. Why was she so desperate to see Annison?

Why did the desire burn in her heart as it did? She'd had a dream, that was all. She had no reason to be there, no sensible excuse for wanting to meet Annison. It was all nonsense, Dreamy Madina lost in a fairy tale once again. What if her parents were worried about her at that very moment? What if they had the neighbors looking for her? She should leave the palace right away and find her way back home.

She intended to go. She really did. But at the very moment when she turned in the direction of the front doors, a man stepped into the hallway from a side room. He was short and had white hair, a full, friendly mouth, and deep laugh lines around his eyes. He wore a dark blue coat with gold buttons and epaulets on his shoulders. Maddy thought he looked like a merry policeman.

"Hello, young lady," he greeted Maddy pleasantly. "Are you lost?"

"No, sir," Maddy replied.

He came closer. "Where are you going?"

"I wanted to go to Annison's chambers," she said honestly, but before she could finish her statement, the man interrupted her.

"Our future queen's chambers? You have business there?"

"I wanted to meet her," Maddy said.

The man seemed distracted, as if he hadn't heard her properly. After a moment he suggested, "If you're going to her chambers, you might be of service to me."

"Me?" she asked.

He scrutinized her briefly. "Only if I can trust you. Can I trust you?"

Maddy nodded vigorously.

He wiggled a finger at her. "Come with me," he instructed.

Maddy followed the man down the main hallway, down
a smaller hallway to a quick left turn, and then down one
more hallway to a door. It led into a small room with a writing desk and long shelves with papers piled up from end to
end. The man bent down behind the desk and arose with a
large vase of flowers. Red and pink carnations, Maddy
thought, and yet they were somehow different from carnations she'd seen at home. Again, the colors seemed brighter,
more intense.

"I would be grateful if you'd take these to her chambers,"
the man said with a gentle smile. "Deliver them to Annison
personally. There's a card for her inside. But when you give
them to her whisper—and I mean *whisper*—that these are
from Simet. Do you understand?"

"I'll give these flowers to her personally and then *whisper*
that they're from Simet," Maddy repeated.

"Good girl," the man said.

"Are you Simet?" Maddy asked.

The man nodded solemnly. "Yes, I am."

"Then why don't you give them to her yourself?"

"For one thing, men are not allowed in those chambers.
For another thing, I don't want anyone else to know these
flowers are from me. It's a great secret that I trust you to keep.
Do you know how to get to Annison's chambers?"

"No, I don't."

Simet chuckled. "I've been working in this palace my
entire life, and I still get lost. Let me show you." Dabbing a
quill pen into a pot of ink, he drew directions from his office
to Annison's chambers. Maddy was glad. She never would have
found them otherwise. "If anyone stops you," Simet added as
he tucked a slip of paper into the pocket on her dress, "just

present this slip of paper and say you have been approved by a lieutenant in the palace guards. That's me."

Maddy took the flowers—they were heavier than she expected—and began her trek through the corridors to Annison's chambers.

CHAPTER THREE

By the time Maddy reached Annison's rooms, her arms hurt from carrying the vase of flowers. In spite of Simet's map, she still got lost once or twice—going down a hall that reached a dead end, walking into rooms filled with people preparing for the evening banquet, and even wandering into the main kitchen. No one seemed to notice her at all, and only one man in a uniform asked to see the slip of paper Simet had given her.

A large, muscular, bald-headed man stood guard at Annison's door. He eyed Maddy with a cool indifference, looked at the slip of paper, then opened the door for her to go in. Maddy's heart quickened a little at the thought of finally seeing Annison, though a part of her still felt like a silly little girl for wanting something so much when there was no apparent reason for wanting it. *It was only a dream*, she thought. *Maybe this is nothing but a dream, too.*

Maddy stood alone in a large room with marble pillars reaching from the floor to a high ceiling. It was simply furnished with a few couches and chairs with large cushions, one or two tables, and velvet curtains that hung around huge, glass doors. The doors led to a balcony that overlooked a mazelike garden. From where Maddy stood in the middle of the room, she could see that the garden was an explosion of greens, reds, yellows, and purples.

Off this main room were several closed doors. Maddy wasn't sure what to do or where to go with the flowers, so she waited a moment, hoping someone would come.

"Well?" a woman's low voice asked.

Maddy was startled. The woman was sitting on one of the couches but was so big and lumpy that Maddy had thought she was a collection of cushions.

"I assume the flowers are not for me," the woman said with a chuckle as she shifted her position and rose from the couch. She had dark hair, which she tucked under a weblike hat, and a full, round face. Her eyes were friendly in spite of the bags that hung like two small purses under them. She had a pug nose and thick lips that made her jowls shake as she spoke. "For Tabby?"

Maddy was so surprised by the appearance of this woman that she didn't know what to say.

"Not for Tabby?" the woman asked, feigning disappointment. "Then I suppose they're for Annison. Give them to me." The woman reached for the vase.

Maddy pulled it away from her. "I was told to give these to Annison personally," she insisted.

"Don't be silly," the woman argued. "I am Tabitha, Annison's nurse. I will see that she gets them."

Maddy refused to hand the flowers over. "I have to give them to Annison myself." Clutching the flowers awkwardly, Maddy pulled Simet's note from her pocket and gave it to Tabby.

Tabby read the note and grunted. "This doesn't mean a thing. This only gives you permission to be here, not to tell *me* who may receive the flowers." She reached for the flowers again.

Maddy stepped back defiantly.

Tabby growled, "Oh, you wicked child!"

"A wicked child?" asked a gentle voice from one of the doorways. "Surely not." To Maddy's delight, it was Annison.

"I say she is," Tabby complained. "She will not give me these flowers for you."

"I was told to give them to you personally," Maddy explained.

"Then you are right not to give them to anyone but me," Annison said with a smile. Again, she looked radiant.

Tabby harumphed.

"But *you*, my dear nurse, are right to be on guard for me," Annison added. "You would have been negligent to allow a strange girl to wander our chambers."

Tabby looked slightly appeased, gave Maddy a final disapproving look, then turned on her heels and left the room.

Annison held out her arms. "Now you may deliver the flowers personally."

Maddy gave her the vase and then, just as Annison was closest to Maddy's face, whispered, "They're from Simet."

Annison's smile widened, but tears filled her eyes. "Oh, I should have known." She placed the flowers on a small pedestal near the glass doors and lingered there, her back to Maddy. The shaking of her shoulders made Maddy realize she was crying.

Maddy went to her and implored, "Please don't cry."

Annison straightened up to compose herself. "I'm not sad," she explained as she wiped her nose with a handkerchief. "I'm happy."

"You don't look very happy."

Annison looked at Maddy and began to cry again. She sat down on one of the couches, burying her face in her handkerchief.

"Oh, dear," Maddy whispered, her heart aching as if the tears were her own. She sat down next to Annison. "I'm here to help you."

Annison looked up at Maddy. "Help me?"

"I had a dream about you, and you asked me to help you, and I promised I would," Maddy explained.

"You dreamt about *me?*"

Maddy nodded.

Annison looked quickly around to make sure no one was near or listening. She leaned close to Maddy and said softly, "Tell me about your dream."

Maddy told her everything: about living in Odyssey, about the dream, about hiding under the porch, and about arriving in time for the king's parade.

As Maddy spoke, Annison's eyes grew wide, and her red lips parted in an expression of awe. "This is wondrous," she concluded.

"I think so, too," Maddy said with a smile. "I'm like Alice in the looking glass. It's magic."

Annison frowned. "I don't know your friend Alice, but no, this isn't magic. At least, not the magic of stories or pagans. This is something more."

Maddy confessed that she didn't understand.

Annison now spoke in a whisper: "It is the Unseen One."

"The what?"

"The Unseen One." Annison suddenly stood up and paced the floor, wringing her hands as she did. "But what does it mean? Why were you sent to me?"

"I came to help you," Maddy reaffirmed.

Annison wasn't listening. She paced and spoke softly, mostly to herself. "I know the stories of old, the writings in the ancient manuscripts that tell of voices, protectors, and messengers who came from other places—strange places—to help us." She suddenly sat next to Maddy again and gazed steadily into her eyes. "But your eyes—they aren't different colors."

Maddy blinked. "Different colors?"

"Oftentimes the ones who came had eyes of two different

colors. But yours are both green. What am I to make of it?"

Maddy felt again as she had when she stood in the crowd: confused and unsure. "I think," she suddenly announced, "that I'm here to help you find your true love."

Annison looked at her, surprised. "What do you mean?"

"Your true love," Maddy replied. "Just like in the stories. You don't love the king, so I'm going to help get you back to your true love."

"You don't know what you're saying," Annison said sharply. "I have no true love."

Maddy was hurt by Annison's tone. "You don't?"

"Has the Unseen One sent you to test me? Or is this a message I must heed?" She paced again. "Is it something cryptic, like a riddle? What do you mean by 'true love'?"

"I mean someone that you *really* love."

"I love no one the way you mean," Annison said simply. "I'm marrying the king."

"But you don't love him," Maddy insisted, though she now doubted herself. "Do you?"

"Love has nothing to do with it," she stated. "I'm doing my duty, for my country." She wrung her hands again. "Oh, I wish I could speak with Simet. He'd know."

"Why can't you?"

"I'm not allowed to see or speak with any men without the king's permission until after the wedding. And to ask to speak with Simet would raise many difficult questions." Annison's face suddenly lit up with an idea. "But *you* can talk to Simet. You can go back to him and tell him what you've told me. Will you do that?"

Maddy shrugged. "If you want me to."

"Then take this." Annison took a ring off her finger. "It's my own. If anyone stops you, show this ring. I am the king's betrothed. No one will harm you as long as you have this ring. It proves that you serve me."

The ring fit on Maddy's thumb. She held it up proudly.

"Beware of one man in particular," Annison then warned. "Lord Hector."

"I've seen him. He doesn't look like a very happy man."

"He isn't. He hates Marus and wants everyone in it to be as miserable as he is." Annison guided Maddy to the door. "Pay close attention to whatever Simet tells you."

"I will." Then Maddy smiled. "You see? I'm going to help you already."

Annison smiled and patted her on the head. "So you are. And I have no doubt that you will help me more than you know. Now go."

Maddy left through the door she'd come in, past the large, bald man, and walked confidently down the hall. Then down another. Then around another. Finally she realized she had wandered into sections of the palace not found on Simet's map. She had no idea where she was going. She stopped a young housemaid and asked for directions. The housemaid rattled out a stream of confusing instructions. Maddy pretended she understood and wandered off again.

Every now and then, she peered out the windows to see if the scene might guide her. It never did. Every view looked different. After another 10 minutes, she stopped at a pair of glass doors that led to a balcony. Outside, three men leaned on the stone handrail, their backs to Maddy. They spoke softly to one another.

"We must strike quickly," one of the men said.

The second man agreed: "If we act even as early as tonight, we may cause enough of a stir to bring the rebellion we need."

"Kill the king right before his wedding? It's a treacherous

idea," the third man observed with a chuckle. His shoulders, covered by a black coat, shook gently.

"Our people will think the Marutians assassinated him to save the dignity of their beloved Annison," the first man added. "It will give our soldiers a cause to rally around—"

"*Someone* to rally around, you mean," the second man interjected.

"Yes. And who might that someone be?" the third man asked knowingly.

"Who else? It must be *you*, my lord," the second man replied. "With the king disposed of, you can legally declare yourself the lord protector. Then, with the allegiance of the army, you can march back to Palatia, arrest the king's brother and heir as a member of the conspiracy, and secure your place on the throne there."

The first man shook his head. "But what about the Marutians?" he objected. "Will they not also rally their forces while Palatia is in turmoil? We risk losing this country after so recently claiming it."

"If a pampered fool like Willem can conquer Marus, I can conquer it again in my sleep," the third man sneered. "Marus is the least of my worries. It's a despicable little country with donkeys for citizens."

"I happen to like it," the first man protested. "And I would be glad to rule it as a reward for my allegiance."

The third man chuckled again. "You haggle even now? You're shrewd, my friend. Yes, if I become lord protector of the kingdom, you may have Marus."

"Good. Maybe I will take Annison as a bride of my own. She's pretty enough."

"If I were you, I would kill her as a member of the conspiracy," the third man advised. "It would show the Marutians that you aren't to be trifled with."

"And what of me, my lord?" the second man asked. "Will you give me Albany as you promised?"

"Albany has always been yours," the third man replied.

"Then let us shake on it," the first man said. "The king's chalice will be poisoned at the banquet tonight by a man in my employ, and you will become lord protector, and we will become the regents of Marus and Albany."

"So be it," the third man agreed.

The first man turned to shake hands with the others. He was a handsome young man with dark hair and a thin goatee. He saw Maddy out of the corner of his eye and spun on her quickly. "Who's this?" he snapped.

The second man, who was older and had sharp features and graying hair, also turned. "What do you want?" he growled.

The third man didn't turn but froze as he was, with his back to Maddy.

"I'm lost," Maddy said nervously.

The young man grabbed her arm roughly. "What did you hear just now?" he demanded.

"Nothing," she stammered. "I only came to ask for your help."

The young man glared at her. "I don't believe you. What did you hear?"

"Nothing," she said more fearfully. He was hurting her arm.

"Ease off, Stephen," the older man said. "She's only a child."

"A child with big ears," Stephen said, lessening his grip on her arm. "Does she have the mouth to match?"

"I'm lost!" Maddy pleaded. "I only want to find the front of the palace."

The older man laughed and told her, "You're well out of your way if you're trying to find the *front* of the palace. Let me tell you how to get there."

"Terrence—" the young man began.

The older man held up his hand to silence him. "How much could she have heard? And who would believe a young girl anyway?" He knelt down closer to Maddy and produced a jewel-handled knife from his belt. "Besides, she wouldn't want her tongue cut out, would she?"

Maddy shook her head. "No, sir."

"Then you will keep your tongue still and go about your business, correct?"

Maddy nodded quickly. "Yes, sir."

The older man kept his eyes fixed on her. "Go down this hallway to the right until it dead-ends, then turn left. Follow that hallway until *it* dead-ends, and then turn right. One right, one left, one right. That will take you to the grand hallway along the front."

"Thank you," Maddy said as she inched away from them.

The older man held up the knife again before tucking it away. "Remember what I said."

"Yes, sir." Maddy didn't waste another second but rushed off down the hall. When she was certain she was out of their reach, she stopped and leaned against the wall. The stone was cool against her hot back. Her face felt flushed, and she thought she might cry. Then she realized, *I've just overheard a plot to kill the king—this very night at the banquet!*

What was she to do? If she told anyone and the man called Terrence found out, he would cut out her tongue. But if she didn't tell anyone, the king would be killed—and Annison, too.

At that moment, she wished she could melt into the wall and somehow go through the other side to her home. This wasn't the fairy tale she wanted to have. This was more like a nightmare.

And she didn't know how to get out of it.

CHAPTER FOUR

"Why are you so pale?" Simet asked when Maddy finally reached him. Even after finding the front doors to the palace, she had needed help from another two servants to get to Simet's office. His brow furrowed with concern. "Is Annison well?"

"She's well, but she wanted me to come back and talk to you," Maddy said. Her mouth clicked from dryness. Simet poured her a cup of water and insisted she drink before continuing. Maddy did, gulping the water down. Then she took a deep breath. "I have to tell you about my dream."

Simet sat on the edge of his desk. "Your dream?"

Maddy looked deeply into his kind eyes and knew she could trust him with anything she had to say. And, like Annison, she believed he would have the answers to help them. So she told him everything she'd told Annison.

Simet listened with a thoughtful expression. He moved only once, and that was to close the door to his office when he feared someone might overhear Maddy's remarkable story.

When Maddy had run out of things to say, he nodded at her. "Yes, this is the work of the Unseen One," he observed.

"I don't know who the Unseen One is," Maddy confessed.

"I'm not surprised to hear it," Simet said sadly. "Only a few of us now acknowledge the Unseen One. Our kings turned their backs on Him and stopped proclaiming Him, so it's little wonder that we've been conquered. And now King Willem is here with his Palatian religion, a religion of man and man's powers, with no room for faith in greater, eternal things. He has already closed our houses of worship. And if Lord Hector had his way, all believers in the Unseen One would be locked up or executed because they deny his religion. Men who do not love the Unseen One often loathe Him and want to wipe any belief in Him from the face of the earth."

"But *who* is the Unseen One?"

Simet scratched his chin as if trying to think of a simple way to explain a complicated idea. Finally he responded, "The Unseen One is the Creator of us all. He is the King of all worlds. He is God over all gods."

"God," Maddy repeated, latching onto a word she understood. "I know about God. I learned about Him in church. And He's all the things you just said."

"Then you know about the Unseen One," Simet said hopefully.

Maddy pondered the idea for a moment. "But I don't remember ever hearing that He took people from one place to another, like He took me from my world to this magic one."

Simet chuckled. "You think this world is magic? The people of this world wouldn't think so. On the contrary, the people of this world would probably consider *your* world magic."

Maddy hadn't thought of it that way. But she stuck by her question. "Still, it seems strange that He brought me from my world to this one."

"It's not for me to guess the ways of the Unseen One. He does as He pleases. And I'm certain the same is true for how He works in your world. No matter how much He has revealed of Himself in our sacred writings, He remains a mystery greater than our finite minds can solve. You're here—that's evidence enough for me that He is at work for some purpose."

"What purpose?" Maddy asked. "What am I doing here?"

"You're not a messenger or a voice or a protector," Simet observed as he looked into her eyes. "But in your dream, you promised you would help Annison. So the Unseen One must have sent you to be her helper."

"I'll help her find her true love," Maddy declared.

Simet looked puzzled. "Whatever do you mean?"

Maddy explained how so many of her favorite stories involved a princess who was in love with a handsome young man but was being forced to marry a mean king. In the end, the handsome young man, who vanquished the mean king, rescued the princess.

"Ah, I see now," Simet said. "But my child, this is not a children's fairy tale. You're not in a story of wishful thinking or fanciful dreams. You're now in a place where the happy endings of childhood give way to the reality of faith."

Maddy looked crestfallen. This was not what she wanted to hear.

Simet patted her arm in comfort. "Dear girl, you wouldn't want to spend your life drinking baby's milk, would you?"

Maddy gazed at him quizzically. "No."

"Well, that's what your fairy tales are," Simet explained. "They're the milk of an innocent faith. But you must never stop at the milk. There comes a time when you must have the nourishment of other things, grown-up things like meat and vegetables. Otherwise you'll never grow as you should. Do you understand?"

Maddy shook her head. "I'm not sure."

"Allow me to try another example." Simet clasped his hands together and looked as if he were in deep thought. Then he continued, "Children's stories and fairy tales often help to light the spark of faith. They help us to see that there are realms much bigger than our own world. They teach us to believe in things we can't understand while they point to other, greater things. But we must eventually fan that spark of faith— allow it to grow into a mature flame that will burn in our hearts throughout our lives."

Maddy didn't reply. It was a lot for her think about.

"You've been brought to us as a helper," Simet went on. "But not to help as a child helps in a fairy tale, with dreamy fantasies of romance, handsome princes, and true love. You're here to help in the raw reality of faith—with sweat and muscle and pain."

Maddy thought again of the dream and of her promise to Annison. Was it possible that the Unseen One had sent her to uncover the plot to kill the king? Even if it meant losing her own tongue? "Sweat and muscle and pain," Maddy repeated softly.

With an unexpected resolve that filled her heart, Maddy knew she could not sit by and allow anything to happen to Annison, no matter what happened to her in the meantime. "There's something else I have to tell you," Maddy said, and then she told Simet about the three men and their plot to poison the king.

Simet's face went white, and he clutched the edge of his desk as if to steady himself. "What did you say the names of the men were?"

"I didn't see who the third man was," she replied. "But the other two were called Stephen and Terrence. The one called Terrence said he would cut my tongue out if I blabbed."

Simet nodded. "There's only one Terrence who would dare do such a thing. But don't fear. He won't have the chance to hurt you. I will see to that."

"Then you'll warn the king?"

Simet hesitated. "No. I think it would be best if *Annison*

warned the king. What better way to show her loyalty and ensure his favor toward her?"

"I don't understand," Maddy admitted, phrasing her question carefully. "If she's from Marus, why is it so important for her to be so chummy with the king?" She thought about it again and quickly added another question. "Why is it Annison's duty to marry someone she doesn't love?"

Simet sighed deeply. "For years we have believed the Unseen One has chosen Annison for a very special place in the destiny of our nation. We were never sure how or what role she would play—not until the day King Willem saw her and decided to marry her. Then we knew. She would marry the king in order to influence him."

"Influence him how?"

"We don't know yet. But it burns in our heart that her role as the queen may make the difference between life and death for many people."

"You keep saying *we*. What *we*?"

"A small gathering of true believers in the Unseen One, including Annison and myself."

Suddenly Maddy thought she understood and gasped, "You're her father!"

Simet smiled. "No, I'm not her father, though she would call me by that name if I allowed it. Her parents were killed when she was a small child, and their wish, written in their will, was that I would raise her in the faith."

"But why is it such a big secret?"

"To protect her. And to protect me. And to protect our gathering of believers. The less anyone knows about us or our connections to one another, the safer we are."

"You're like a secret club?"

"Something like that. But our secret is a dangerous one.

Under the kings of Marus, we were frowned upon for keeping our faith in the Unseen One. Under King Willem—or I should say, under *Lord Hector*—we could lose our lives."

"But that means the king is marrying a believer in the Unseen One and he doesn't even know it."

Simet smiled again. "Exactly."

A knock came at the door, and then it was pushed open without an invitation. Lord Hector himself peered in. He looked at Simet first and said, "Simet, I want to discuss the security for this evening's banquet." Then he saw Maddy, and a flash of surprise lit up his eyes for a second and then disappeared. "Forgive my intrusion," he added quickly.

"Not at all, my lord," Simet replied.

"Then come to the Great Hall. I wish a word with you and the other guards."

"Yes, my lord."

Lord Hector glanced at Maddy again and then turned to leave. In the moment he did so, Maddy noticed the back of his black coat and the shape of his shoulders, and she knew. "It was him," she whispered after the door was closed and she heard his retreating footsteps.

"What's that?" Simet asked.

"He was the third man on the balcony."

"Lord *Hector*? In a plot to poison the king?"

"Yes."

"Are you sure, Maddy? You must be completely sure."

"Yes. He wants to do it so he can take over Palatia."

Simet looked like a man who had suddenly found the last two pieces to a jigsaw puzzle. "I've often wondered about him. I've watched how he speaks to the king, the look in his eyes. He's a man who covets power. So I should not be surprised."

"Shall I go back to Annison now?"

"Yes, hurry and tell her what you know."

Maddy stood up and went to the door. Just as her hand touched the knob, Simet added earnestly, "Maddy, you've been sent to help us, and help us you have. But I don't think your part in this drama is finished. You must keep your eyes and ears open. Assume nothing about what you see and hear. Report *everything* to Annison or to me. Do you understand?"

Maddy nodded, suddenly feeling very important.

CHAPTER FIVE

→———←

The royal banquet to celebrate the forthcoming marriage of King Willem and Annison was a lavish affair. Hundreds of dignitaries and noblemen from Palatia, along with the well-to-do of Marus, crowded into the Great Hall. The men wore frilly lace collars and matching coats and trousers of deep blue, light green, or gold that seemed to sparkle. The women wore velvet or silk dresses, each with elaborate designs of flowers, birds, or stripes, some with colorful shawls draped over their shoulders. Many of the women *and* men wore wigs that rose up from their heads in piles like cotton candy or bird's nests. Those women who didn't wear wigs had their hair done in large curls. The men favored long hair, carefully combed and kept in place by what looked to Maddy like oil or wax.

The guests took their places at the many tables, now set with white linen, plates of china, and solid silver cutlery. Blazing torches shone from wall sconces in between colorful tapestries that had been hung for the occasion. Candles were lit at every setting, giving the entire hall a yellow tint. The chandeliers, also alight with candles, looked like clusters of stars, ready to explode over them all.

Enormous trays of food were brought out by the palace servants—seven courses in all—and served to the many guests. The room was an intoxicating mix of smells. Considering the number of guests, Maddy was impressed by the speed with which the servants did their work. They began as the sun set and continued serving well past 11:00.

The king and Annison sat side by side at the head table.

For tonight, the king didn't wear a wig but combed his ginger-colored hair forward in a style that reminded Maddy of a picture of Julius Caesar she'd once seen at school. Annison was dressed discreetly in a simple pink gown with fringes of lace and bowed ribbons attached to them. To the royal couple's left and right were Lord Hector, who still looked bored, and several other men and women Maddy didn't know. Stephen and Terrence were at the head table, too, and kept looking at each other anxiously. As a member of Annison's court, Maddy was given a seat at a table in the corner nearest the head table. She sat next to Tabby, who ate with great enthusiasm.

Maddy was too nervous to eat. Ever since reporting her news to Annison, she had been on a knife's-edge of suspense, wondering how the evening would play out.

Near midnight, flasks of a sweet, red drink were poured into the guests' chalices. It was time for the royal toast, and now Maddy found herself sitting on the edge of her seat. She had told Annison of the plot to poison the king, but she had no idea what Annison had done with the information or how she had passed the word to the king. She watched Stephen and Terrence, who watched the king's every move. Lord Hector maintained his usual bored expression.

The king stood up, raising high his chalice—a large goblet with green and red jewels around its sides. "Ladies and gentlemen," he said in his booming voice, "I am grateful for your attendance tonight. To honor the occasion, I promised my betrothed that I would not make a lengthy speech."

A titter of laughter worked its way through the crowd.

"It is enough for me to say thank you to all, to wish prosperity on the united kingdoms of Palatia and Marus, and to invite you back in a week's time for the wedding."

The crowd responded with scattered applause.

"Now for the royal toast," he announced.

There was a rustling throughout the room as all the guests stood by their chairs and raised their chalices.

"To my betrothed, the future queen," he stated happily.

"To the future queen!" the crowd responded.

Maddy watched the king, her eyes growing wider and wider. The chalice moved toward his lips. Annison remained seated and still, her face betraying nothing but her usual shyness at being the center of attention. Had Annison not told him about the poison? Was the plot to kill him going to succeed?

"My king!" Lord Hector suddenly shouted from his place.

The king hesitated, the chalice only an inch from his lips. "Lord Hector?" he asked, lowering the cup.

"Do not drink from that chalice," Lord Hector warned.

The king looked puzzled. "This is most unusual, Hector. It's the royal toast. Why shouldn't I?" he inquired.

"Because, on this very day, I have uncovered a plot to assassinate Your Majesty—by poison in that very chalice."

The crowd, shocked, stood where they were, many not sure how to react. Several of the noblemen instinctively drew their swords. Maddy's jaw dropped. What kind of game was Hector playing? Why would he stop the plot that he had helped to mastermind?

Stephen and Terrence watched Hector with bewilderment on their faces. Maddy noticed that Terrence's hand subtly moved to his belt, his hand resting on the handle of his knife.

The king remained composed. "And who would dare to attempt such an assassination?"

"Two trusted men in your very midst," Lord Hector announced, then pointed dramatically. "Stephen and Terrence!"

Suddenly the palace guards burst through the doors, including Simet, and rushed to the head table. Stephen held up his hands in surrender, but Terrence pulled out his knife and lunged at the king.

Lord Hector was quicker, though, and leapt between the two men. He also had a knife in his hand—Maddy had no idea where it had come from—which he thrust into Terrence's chest. They both fell to the ground, disappearing behind the ornate tablecloth. Seconds later, Lord Hector reappeared and dusted himself off as if he had merely tripped over something.

The crowd erupted in shouts and applause.

There was a commotion at the back of the hall as two guards grabbed one of the servants. Maddy assumed it was the one the conspirators had hired to poison the drink.

Simet and the other guards had grabbed Stephen, who offered no resistance. He now leered at Lord Hector. "I should have known," he growled over and over as they dragged him out of the hall.

"Well done, Lord Hector!" the king said happily once the offenders had been removed. His eyes danced and his cheeks were apple red from the excitement. He raised his chalice again. "I salute you!"

And then, to everyone's horror, he gulped down his drink.

"Your Majesty!" Hector cried out.

The king slammed the chalice down on the table and laughed. "You are quick, Lord Hector, but my beloved Annison is quicker. She was already privy to the traitors' plot to poison me, and I made sure to change chalices. Little did they realize that had we drunk our toast, both Stephen and Terrence would have fallen dead from their own poison, which I had placed in their cups!"

Lord Hector bowed in homage to Annison. "Our new queen is a remarkable woman," he said smoothly. "I wonder, if I may ask, how she knew of the plot?"

"We women have our ways," Annison replied pleasantly.

Lord Hector forced himself to smile. "I have no doubt that you do."

For an instant, Annison's eyes caught Maddy's, and she winked at her.

The attending maidens in Annison's chambers were abuzz with what had happened at the banquet. They speculated about how Annison had learned of the plot and if there were any others involved who weren't caught, and then they told and retold the dramatic moment when the king nearly drank the chalice—and then did, to everyone's surprise.

"What a joke!" one said.

"How brave of the king," another observed.

Only after Tabby threatened them with hard chores the next day if they didn't go to bed *that minute* did the chattering stop.

Maddy was given a small bedroom off Annison's main bedroom and a wardrobe of day and night clothes. She had no idea how Annison managed it, but the clothes were all the right size. Maddy slipped into a nightgown and snuggled into the soft down mattress, but she was too excited to sleep, her mind counting unanswered questions like sheep. She thought she heard a sound from Annison's room and decided to sneak a peek to see if Annison had gone to bed. She hadn't; the bed was empty. A gentle breeze blew the pale curtains back and forth. The glass doors leading to the balcony were open, and Maddy could see Annison's silhouette pacing outside. Maddy crossed the room and stopped at the doorway.

Annison had her eyes closed and seemed to be talking to

herself. Maddy realized she was praying. "Thank You" was all Maddy heard her say. And then Annison opened her eyes and gazed peacefully at Maddy.

"You should be asleep," Annison chided gently, gathering her robe close around her as if warding off a chill. But the night was warm, crickets chirped somewhere below, and pale moonlight filled the clear sky.

"Oh, look!" Maddy gasped, her eyes fixed on the light overhead. There in the sky was a bright moon—and right next to it, a little smaller and more orange, was *another* moon. "You have two moons!"

Annison glanced up at them. "Yes, we do. How many do you have in your world?" she asked.

"Just one," Maddy replied. The sight mesmerized her. *Imagine having two moons in your world,* she thought in amazement. She stood looking at the double orbs for a few moments.

Annison watched her, a tiny smile betraying her affection for Maddy. "You remind me of someone," Annison observed.

"Who?"

"Me."

Maddy turned to her, an unformed question on her lips.

"I once looked at the world with the wonder you have. I believed in fairy tales and happy endings."

"You don't now?"

"In my heart, I still do," she said warmly. "But I've also learned a great deal about the world, and sometimes the happy endings don't come the way we think they should. But they come eventually, beyond this world, thanks to the Unseen One."

"Simet told me I'm not here to help you find your true love. He said I need to help you the way the Unseen One wants me to help you. He said I need to grow up."

"We all have to grow up, it's true. But that doesn't mean we must lose our sense of wonder and awe. The mystery of faith is too great for that. Even now I look around me—at the beauty of those two moons, at the secrets of the stars, even at the extraordinary way you have come to me—and I realize there's so much I don't understand. But I know what I must do."

"You'll marry King Willem."

"Yes, I will."

Saying his name reminded Maddy of the drama at the banquet and her many questions about it. "I can't figure out what happened," she stated. "Lord Hector was one of the men who plotted to kill the king, but then he turned on Stephen and Terrence at the last minute."

"Lord Hector is a shrewd and cunning man. I suspect he knew somehow that their plans had been found out. He must have decided to turn it to his advantage."

Maddy remembered how Lord Hector had come into Simet's office when Maddy was there. It was possible that he'd seen her on the balcony or recognized her voice and assumed she would tell Simet what she'd heard in spite of Terrence's threat. "But you told the king that Lord Hector was one of the men, didn't you?" she asked.

"No, I didn't."

"Why not?"

"It's one thing to accuse underlings like Stephen and Terrence of treason," she replied. "It's another thing to accuse the king's most-trusted adviser. I would have needed more proof than your word to persuade the king to take action against Lord Hector. As it is, this will warn him to be careful."

Maddy felt uneasy at the thought. If Lord Hector knew that Maddy had told Simet and Annison about his plans, wouldn't he want revenge against her? Maddy gave it some thought but decided not to say anything to Annison. She was there to help her, not add to her worry.

"I think it's time for bed," Annison suddenly announced. "We have a lot to do tomorrow."

"What am I going to do?" Maddy asked.

Annison smiled at her. "You'll help me to prepare for the wedding, and perhaps you'll be my eyes and ears in other parts of the palace. We'll see."

CHAPTER SIX

Preparing for the wedding was an enormous task, far more complicated than Maddy would have ever thought. There were flowers to be ordered, dresses to be made, food to be chosen for the reception afterward, seating arrangements to be secured for the wedding itself and the reception, an order of service for the ceremony to be decided upon, a schedule to be devised for the royal "ride" from the palace to the royal chapel (where the wedding would take place), a procession through Sarum to be planned, and on and on.

For most of the day after the banquet, Maddy sat next to Annison, scribbling her dictation of things that needed to be seen to in the days leading up to the wedding. Then, shortly after lunchtime, Tabby entered the main room of the chambers and whispered something to Annison. Annison nodded quickly and signaled Maddy to follow her into one of the side rooms. After they entered, Annison closed the door.

The room appeared to be some kind of study, with squares of dark paneling covering three of the walls. A fireplace took up most of the fourth. In the center were a writing desk and small tables holding a selection of books and decorative items like china vases and busts. The floor was covered with a large, colorful rug.

"Is something wrong?" Maddy asked.

"I have an errand for you to run," Annison replied. She went to the fireplace and tugged at a small piece of marble that hung like an icicle from the side. Suddenly a panel on the wall behind them opened a couple of inches.

"A secret door?" Maddy asked, amazed.

Annison pressed a hand against Maddy's back to urge her forward. "Simet has worked in this palace most of his life," she explained. "He knows every inch of it, including the secret passageways. He told me about this the day I moved in."

"Where does it go?"

"It leads to many different rooms. But—" Annison pulled a piece of paper from her sleeve and handed it to Maddy. "Follow this map and these directions. They'll take you to the king's reception room."

"You want me to spy on the king?"

"Lord Hector is about to have an audience with King Willem to discuss what happened at the banquet last night. I need to know what he says."

Maddy took a step into the passageway but stopped. "It's dark," she complained.

Annison reached up and grabbed something on the inside wall. It was a torch that, from the smell, must have been doused in oil. Using flint from the fireplace, she lit the torch. Its flame was small but adequate. She gave the torch to Maddy. "Don't get lost this time," Annison teased her.

Maddy giggled and stepped into the passageway. The torch surrounded her with moving shadows.

Annison gestured to a small lever on the wall. "This will open the panel to let you back in," she informed her.

"Okay," Maddy said.

Annison closed the panel door.

Maddy moved forward slowly until she was sure of her footing and of the passage's width. It was surprisingly wide. Following the instructions, she crossed several side passages, then turned right and passed more doorways with levers. She wondered where they all led to and imagined the trouble she'd cause if she suddenly appeared in one of the rooms. Counting the doorways carefully, she turned left after the eighth door and walked for a long time before she found the passage Annison had marked on the map. She turned left again and followed it until it reached a dead end. There she found a hook in the wall to hold the torch.

The map indicated that she wouldn't find a lever on the wall but a small knob, which she was to slide carefully to one side. She did. It opened a small, rectangular peephole. She found herself looking at a large room with a throne sitting on a small stage. Large, velvet curtains surrounded it. Empty chairs stretched out from the foot of the stairs in two rows. King Willem suddenly appeared through a door behind the stage and walked casually to the throne, where he sat down and inspected his fingernails, then adjusted the sleeves on his coat.

A moment later, a large double door opened and Lord Hector strode in. He was dressed in the same mournful-looking black coat and trousers. He stood at the foot of the stage and bowed stiffly.

"Your Majesty," he intoned.

"My dear Lord Hector," the king greeted, waving him forward. "Good day to you, and thank you once again for your chivalry on my behalf."

Lord Hector dipped his head and cleared his throat as if embarrassed. "Yes, of course, my liege," he began. "Now—to business?"

"If you must."

Lord Hector clasped his hands behind his back and announced, "I have interrogated Stephen and his treasonous servant in the dungeon."

"In your usual meticulous manner, I have no doubt."

"Yes, sire. Sadly, neither was made of strong stuff, and they expired in the process."

"How sad," the king said without meaning it. "Oh, well, I didn't really want to execute them in the week of my wedding anyway."

Maddy put a hand over her mouth. The easygoing way that the two men spoke about death appalled her.

"Did you learn anything valuable?" the king asked.

"The conspiracy to overthrow you is far-reaching."

The king raised an eyebrow. "Is it?"

"I was able to learn that Stephen, Terrence, and the servant they employed to poison your chalice are all part of that terrible cult I've warned you about."

"Cult? "

"The believers of the Old Faith."

"Oh, that nonsense about the Unseen One and all that."

"Exactly."

Maddy couldn't believe what she was hearing. Did Lord Hector really think he could get away with such a lie?

"I thought you outlawed that when we arrived." The king crossed his legs and leaned back comfortably into his throne.

"I did, sire," Lord Hector replied without any variation in the drone of his voice. "But their members still meet secretly, as evidenced by the cunning plan they nearly succeeded with last night."

"It's curious, though."

"Sire?"

"I had always understood that the believers in the Old Faith were nonviolent," the king said. "All they've ever wanted is to be able to worship that strange God of theirs as they saw fit. Why would they want to kill me?"

Lord Hector answered as if teaching a child. "You are a

Palatian, sire. The members of the Old Faith are Marutians. In matters of national honor and identity, even the most-peaceful cults will resort to violence if they feel they have no other choice."

"Then why don't we let them worship the way they want and be done with them? They have no complaint against me if I grant them that."

Lord Hector shook his head slowly. "Because it won't end there, sire. Their faith is bound up in the destiny of this nation. If you allow them to worship freely, it will be no time at all before their faith will spill over to the people at large. And once that has happened, there will be a trickle, then a river, and finally a flood of patriotism. With that patriotism will come patriotic acts—against you, to free themselves from your rule. History has shown it to be true time and again."

"Oh, dear!"

"I have outlawed the Old Faith to hold back the tide of their zeal," Lord Hector explained. "And, frankly, I find it offensive. For them to superstitiously believe in ancient gods when it's clear that *we* are the keepers of our fate, the champions of our destiny, is ignorance at its worst. I cannot tolerate it."

"As usual, you speak eloquently and poetically," the king said appreciatively. "What do you propose?"

"I propose that outlawing the Old Faith isn't enough. We must use our forces to come down on them like a hammer. We must drive them from their hiding places and arrest them."

The king sighed wearily. "If you insist. But be discreet about it. I don't want a lot of fuss distracting from my wedding day."

"Of course, sire." Lord Hector bowed and walked away.

Maddy waited a moment to see what the king would do next. He sat, yawned, and inspected his fingernails again. Then the door opened and a page stepped in.

"The mayor of Sarum to see you, sire," he announced.

The king waved a hand at the page. "See him in," he commanded, barely stifling his boredom.

Maddy closed the peephole and stepped back into the passageway. She felt numbed by what she'd just heard. Lord Hector was actually placing the blame for the assassination attempt on the believers in the Unseen One! It made her blood boil to think about it.

She had to hurry back and tell Annison. Retrieving the torch, she rushed down the passageway in the direction from which she had come. She followed the map carefully while moving as fast as she could. Then, as she passed one particular side passage, she thought she heard footsteps. They were terribly close to her, but she didn't see a light.

I hope there's nobody else in here, she worried.

She pressed on, quickening her step.

A harsh sound, like a loud, throaty cough, made her stop in her tracks. It was unmistakably human. Someone was in the passageway with her.

She looked around quickly, her torch throwing very little light into the shadows. Should she call out? *No,* she thought. *Keep moving. Don't stop for anything. And try not to be afraid.*

But the fear seized her anyway, and she misread the map once or twice, winding up down the wrong passageway or stuck at a dead end.

Still, she was certain that someone was nearby. She thought she heard heavy breathing off to the left. And there was the clear sound of a heel scuffing against the stone floor somewhere off to her right. Was she being followed, or was her imagination playing tricks on her?

Finally she arrived at the last passage that would take her back to Annison's chambers. She sprinted the length of it, gasping with relief when she got to the lever. But just as she reached for it, a pale, white hand shot out of the darkness and grabbed her wrist.

She started to scream, but another hand clamped down over her mouth. Wide-eyed, she looked up into the face of Lord Hector.

"I've often wondered if there were rats in these passageways," he hissed softly. "Now I see that there are."

Maddy tried to tell him to let go, but he kept his hand firm.

"I haven't been able to figure you out, little girl," he growled. "Are you a spy for someone? Or do you just have the uncanny luck of being in the right places at the wrong time? Which is it?"

He didn't remove his hand for her to answer.

"One moment you're singing in a children's choir, and the next you're an unwanted guest on a balcony. One moment I see you talking to Simet—and I can guess the subject—and then, like magic, you're a member of Annison's court. It mystifies me. And I'm not a man who mystifies easily. Are you working for Simet or for Annison—or is there some connection between the two of them I don't know about? *Who are you*, little girl?"

He still didn't take his hand away.

He leaned his face so close that she could smell cabbage on his breath. "I have many questions about you. And I want you to know that, one way or the other, I *will* find the answers. It's only because I'm not sure about you that I'm going to let you go." He finally released his grip on her. "But if you're the rat I think you are, *you will be exterminated.* Consider it a warning." He paused to correct himself. "No. Consider it a threat."

With that said, he stepped back into the shadows and seemed to disappear.

Maddy waited to hear his retreating footsteps. Her heart raced, her breath came in short gasps, and those were the only sounds she heard. When she was certain he was gone, she pulled the lever and stumbled into the study.

CHAPTER SEVEN

Maddy told Annison about Lord Hector's plans to arrest the believers in the Old Faith. She also described what had happened with him in the passageway.

Annison was concerned but reassuring. "Lord Hector is clever enough to be careful with you," she said soothingly. "He won't do anything to you as long as he can't figure out who you're working for and why. For all he knows, you may be working for the king himself."

"But he threatened me," Maddy reminded her.

"To *scare* you," Annison replied. "All it means is that we must be careful. We must trust no one. We may be surrounded by his spies."

Annison then sent Maddy to tell all the news to Simet.

On the way to Simet's office, Maddy was on edge, sure that everyone she encountered worked as a spy for Lord Hector. By the time she reached Simet, she was in a cold sweat.

"We don't want to turn you into a nervous wreck," Simet said sympathetically. "I think we must establish a secret routine, a set time in a secret place where I'll meet you and we can swap messages. Otherwise you may well be followed if you keep coming to me more than once a day."

"Where and when?" Maddy asked.

Simet thought about it, then suggested, "There's a door leading to the old bell tower on the east side of the palace. It's dark, with a private courtyard that no one uses anymore. Better still, there are no windows or doors nearby from which anyone can spy on us."

"I don't know where it is."

Simet smiled. "As usual, I'll draw you a map. But you must memorize the directions and then destroy it. The less we have in writing, the better." Simet quickly drew the map and handed it to Maddy. "Let's meet every evening at six. In case of an emergency, leave one of Annison's smaller scarves tied to my office doorknob. Then I'll know to meet you right away."

"But what about Lord Hector's plans?" Maddy asked.

"I'll inform the other believers in the Old Faith of his devious plans."

Everyone was so busy over the next few days with the wedding details that they hardly noticed when Lord Hector sent out a proclamation to the palace staff. It said:

"As an oath of allegiance to the king and his queen, all members of the royal staff must sign a declaration of loyalty, renouncing any duty, obligation, or fealty to any other faiths, powers, or provinces. Signed, Lord Hector, Chancellor to King Willem IV of Palatia, Marus, and Albany."

"It's a test," Annison observed when Maddy brought the proclamation to her attention. "Lord Hector wants to see if he can trick any of the true believers into the open. Fortunately, with the chaos surrounding the wedding, I don't believe he'll be able to force everyone to sign the proclamation. As it is, I will insist that my court be exempt. Lord Hector has no authority over me. Only the king can force us to obey."

"Will you sign if the king makes you?"

"No," Annison replied. "And let us hope the king does not try."

The situation was far more difficult for Simet, however, as

Maddy discovered when she spoke to him at the bell tower that night.

"He's a cunning devil," Simet observed. He was more agitated than Maddy had ever seen him. "The audacity of the man, to insist on allegiance when he himself wants to kill the king!"

"But what will you do?" Maddy asked, growing worried for this man who had fast become a good friend.

"As a true believer, I cannot—*will not*—sign such a proclamation."

"Then how will you get out of it?"

Simet tapped a finger along the side of his chin for a moment, then responded, "I can't. I can only hope to stall him until he becomes so busy with other things that he forgets who signed and who didn't."

"I don't think Lord Hector is the kind of man who'd forget," Maddy said forlornly.

"Me, either," Simet agreed with a frown. Then, as if to wave away the worry that hung like cobwebs over them, he continued, "One night soon after the wedding, I want to take you to one of our meetings."

"Of the true believers?"

"Yes. I want them to meet you, to see with their own eyes a helper from the Unseen One."

Maddy suddenly felt shy. "I won't have to make a speech or anything, will I?"

"No, of course not."

"Good."

"I'll let you know when," Simet said, then urged, "You must go back. Tell Annison that she's in my thoughts and prayers as we approach the wedding day. The Unseen One will bless her for her faithfulness to her duty."

As Maddy left the courtyard, she thought she saw someone or something move in a dark shadow near the palace wall. She watched for a moment, her heart racing. A few seconds later, a cat meowed and strolled into the open. Maddy breathed a sigh of relief and strolled on, trying to appear casual.

Simet emerged a moment later, his thoughts consumed by Lord Hector's proclamation. He was oblivious to anything unusual about the small courtyard. Had he been paying closer attention, he would have seen the same cat move back into the shadows—and rub itself against a man's leg.

The wedding day of King Willem and Annison finally arrived. It nearly made Maddy's adventure seem like a fairy tale again. The sun shone bright, and the sky was a rich blue. Annison, dressed in a long, white, silk gown with headdress and veil, looked again like a princess. She was taken to the chapel in a large, gold-trimmed coach, which drove first around the major roads of the city so the people could cheer her. They did, with an enthusiasm Maddy hoped was heartfelt and not forced by soldiers in the crowd. The king went directly from his palace chambers to the chapel.

Maddy, Tabby, and the other members of Annison's court were also dressed in white dresses of lace and silk and transported to the chapel in a special black-and-silver, open-topped wagon.

The chapel, normally a cold and austere place, came alive with the colors of the many flowers brought in for the occasion. Maddy thought the smell was heavenly. She noticed that Lord Hector, still dressed in black, clenched a handkerchief to his nose as if the smell were offensive to him.

Simet was there as well, dressed in his best uniform of dark blue, with gold buttons and epaulets. He clutched a blue, tri-cornered hat to his chest and occasionally pulled a lace hand-kerchief from his sleeve to dab his forehead as if he were hot. But Maddy noticed that it was a ploy. He was secretly signaling Annison, who also tucked and untucked a handkerchief from her own sleeve. Maddy imagined that they were expressing their love for each other. Or maybe Simet was reminding Annison to be brave while she did her duty. Whatever it was, Annison seemed to straighten up, a look of resolve in her eyes. Maddy then saw tears in Simet's eyes.

The king was dressed in a brilliant gold coat and trousers, with silk stockings and gold shoes. He wore another wig, this one blond, but it looked more like a hat than anything hairlike.

The wedding ceremony itself was a disappointment to Maddy. Once the bridegroom and bride came together at the altar, the words of the service became legalistic. Maddy thought it sounded more like the two of them were signing a contract than getting married.

"This is so unromantic," Maddy whispered to Tabby at one point. "It looks like a fairy tale, but it sounds like a business meeting."

Tabby rolled her eyes in an annoyed fashion and whis-pered back, "Palatians aren't known for romance. This is how they conduct their weddings. I think they're long and tedious. It would be even longer if they hadn't cut out any semblance of the old religious service. Good riddance to it, I say."

Annison had told Maddy that, though Tabby was loyal to Annison, she wasn't a believer in the Old Faith. She considered it a lot of superstitious nonsense. So they had to be careful what they said around her. Maddy often wondered why Tabby, a Marutian, had gone against the traditions of her ancestors and given up on the Unseen One, but she never dared to ask.

Two long hours went by with exchanges of vows, of documents, of rings, of scepters, of crowns, and of other symbolic things Maddy lost track of. After the formal ceremony finished, everyone returned to the palace grounds for another banquet, this time under several pavilions on the grounds.

Everything about the banquet was as wonderful as the banquet they'd had the week before, except no one tried to poison the king this time. Many speeches were made by visiting dignitaries, and the king himself—half drunk, Maddy thought—gave an hour-long speech that declared his love for Annison, his hopes for the kingdom, and his optimism about the future.

The sun set, the two moons rose, and the king and queen left by the king's golden carriage to tour the city once more and wave to those who came out to greet them. Then they went off to somewhere in Palatia—a secret place belonging to the king—for their month-long honeymoon.

With Annison gone, Annison's court now had to move all her belongings to rooms next to the king's own chambers. Maddy asked Tabby why they still had separate rooms now that they were married. Tabby rolled her eyes and quickly explained that it was Palatian custom for the queen to have her own rooms apart from the king's, and then he could summon her when he wanted her. Maddy still didn't understand and persisted in questioning the arrangement until Tabby impatiently told her to mind her own business and go back to work. Maddy shrugged and obeyed.

The queen's court was busy from morning until night, packing Annison's things and filling trunks with her clothes, jewelry, and personal mementos.

On the third evening, a grandfather clock in the corner

struck six, and Maddy suddenly remembered that she hadn't been to the bell tower since before the wedding. She had assumed there was no reason for her to meet Simet while Annison was away since there were no messages to send. But suddenly she doubted her assumption and thought she should slip away to make certain all was well with Simet.

It had rained most of the day, but now the sun came out just in time to set. Pools of water lay around the courtyard like large footprints. Simet was waiting for her just inside the bell-tower door. "You came after all," he said without reproach.

Maddy felt ashamed. "I'm sorry," she apologized. "I assumed we wouldn't meet while Annison was on her honeymoon. I should have asked you first."

"Don't worry," he offered with a smile. His face was half shadowed by the dusk, but she saw his eyes darting quickly around the courtyard.

"Is something wrong?"

"We're going to meet the true believers."

"*Tonight?*" she asked. "Right now?"

"Now," he answered and gently took her arm. "Come with me."

Simet guided her across the courtyard to an outer wall that ran along the palace grounds. The grass was squishy and wet. In a few minutes, they reached a small, wooden door. He pulled a key from a loop on his belt and unlocked it. They stepped through into a wooded area. Simet stopped and made sure to lock the door again behind them.

"This way," he said, and she followed him through the woods until they reached an alley shrouded by old buildings of timber and stone. They crept along until the alley reached a larger street. People, horses, and wagons made their way in opposite directions on the two sides of the street. Simet seemed determined to lose them both in the congestion. Once or twice Maddy worried that she would get separated from him, but he always reached out to take her hand or her arm so she wouldn't get lost.

The entire way, Maddy wondered what to expect from the group of true believers. Would there be magic or miracles? Would something marvelous happen because she was with them? Maybe the Unseen One would somehow appear to them.

They ducked down another alley and wound up in a small court of townhouses. The Tudor-style beams, crooked door-ways, and angled windows peered at them. Large boxes filled with flowers stretched along the windows and at the base of each house. Simet directed Maddy to a door on the far right, where he tapped on it in a rhythm that reminded Maddy of Morse code. A spy hole opened briefly, then closed again, and the latch lifted on the inside of the door. It was opened by a small, silver-haired woman with a skeletal face. She smiled when she saw Maddy.

"Oh, dear girl, come in," she greeted and gestured with a bony finger. "Come in, Simet." She looked cautiously out the door again and then closed it quickly. They stood in a dark hall-way for a moment until she moved around them. "In here," she instructed and led them to a room at the far end of the hall. It was a modest sitting room with a sofa and divan, one or two end tables, a carpet with pink and blue flowers in it, and thick, blue curtains over the windows. The woman stooped and suddenly pulled the carpet back. "They're waiting," she said.

"Aren't you joining us, Annigua?" Simet asked her.

She shook her head vigorously. It seemed so fragile that Maddy thought it might fall off. "It's my turn to keep watch."

Simet knelt and grabbed hold of a small ring inset into a

floorboard Maddy hadn't noticed. He gave it a tug and a trap-door lifted up. The old woman took it from him and held it while he stepped onto unseen stairs in the rectangular dark-ness. Maddy carefully followed him.

At the bottom of the stairs was a large room, cool like a cel-lar but decorated in comfortable-looking chairs. Oil lamps were lit and hung from the beams crossing the ceiling. Banners on the walls contained symbols Maddy had never seen before. A small group of men and women was gathered in the center. The people were on their knees and looked as if they'd been praying. One man rose to greet them. He was a stocky, with a round, pudgy face, salt-and-pepper beard, and mostly gray hair pulled back in a ponytail.

"Simet," the man said pleasantly, then turned his gaze to Maddy. "And you are Maddy."

"Yes, sir."

"I am Petrad."

"He's the elder of our group," Simet added quickly.

The rest of the group now stood. Petrad introduced each man and woman to Maddy, but they were a blur of names and faces. Once the formalities were over, they drew the chairs into a circle and sat down. Maddy was aware of everyone staring at her, but she tried to ignore it, choosing instead to look at her hands folded in her lap.

"What's the latest news from the palace?" Petrad asked Simet.

"Hector is putting more pressure on some of us to sign his oath of allegiance. He has cornered me twice about it."

"What did you say to him?"

"I told him that the oath was buried in a stack of papers in my office and I would get to it when I could. I suggested it wasn't a priority over my many other duties for the king."

"Did he accept that?"

"He gave me that cold look that only he gives so well. I don't know how much longer I can put him off. In any event, I don't trust him. I believe this oath is a first step to bigger things. He wants us annihilated."

"So he does. He's already sending his soldiers to the homes of suspected members." Petrad pursed his lips as if his statement brought back a painful memory. All he said, though, was "We will continue to pray for you and the others."

"Thank you."

Suddenly they all lowered their heads, and Petrad prayed to the Unseen One to give Simet strength and guidance in his role at the palace. Maddy watched out of the corner of her eyes, wondering if something bizarre or exciting would happen. Then they lifted their heads again.

"And what about you, Maddy?" Petrad asked. Maddy looked at him. "Do you have any messages for us from the Unseen One?"

The question scared her. "No, I don't think so."

Petrad smiled. "I just thought I'd ask. Meanwhile, is there anything we can do for you?"

Maddy shrugged. "For me? I don't think so."

"Tell me: How is your faith?" he asked.

"My faith?" She was feeling more confused.

"Yes. Tell us the condition of your soul."

"Oh, don't be ridiculous, Petrad!" a woman with a scarf on her head said sharply. "She's a young girl. 'Condition of your soul,' indeed. You can't expect her to know what you're talking about."

"Then *you* ask her, Bridga," Petrad insisted.

The woman called Bridga smiled at Maddy. "You came to Annison as a helper from another world, which is a wondrous thing to us," she explained. "But Simet tells us you are unsure of your faith."

"I am?" she asked. She couldn't figure out what they were getting at.

"He suggested that you think you may be in a dream or a fairy tale," said the woman.

Maddy looked at Simet helplessly. He gave her an embarrassed wink and spread his hands in resignation.

"I see what you mean," Maddy began. She tried to form an answer. "I think ... I understand now that this isn't a fairy tale. What I mean to say is that I wasn't very happy that Annison had to marry the king when she didn't love him. But she did it anyway. Out of duty to the Unseen One. I guess that's how it happens sometimes. Real life isn't always a fairy tale, but sometimes ..." Maddy paused, unsure of her words or how to finish her thought. Finally she said, "What I mean is, when I grow up, I hope to be as brave and courageous as Annison is."

The group seemed to approve. Petrad clapped his hands together. "Well said! Bravo!"

Bridga looked at Maddy earnestly, but she had a faraway look in her eyes. "The time will come soon when you *will* have to be as brave and courageous as Annison," she suggested. "Perhaps more so. But you must give up your ideas of magic tricks."

Maddy's mouth went dry. "What do you mean?"

"You're still thinking as a child," she said. "Even now you want magic tricks from the Unseen One. You hope to be amazed and astonished, like a member of an audience watching a magic play. But the Unseen One does not stand on the center of this stage. He watches from the wings while *you* play your part. Do not wait for magic and miracles, dear child. Play your part and play it well. That's what you're here to do."

The group was silent now. Maddy felt the heat of their watchful eyes. She didn't know how the woman called Bridga had known to say what she said, but she was right. Maddy was still thinking like a child.

Just then a small bell on the far wall rang. The men and women leapt to their feet, leaving Maddy to sit, unsure of what was happening.

"We have guests," Simet said softly, coming close to Maddy

"Guests?" Maddy asked.

Simet put a finger to his lips. "We must be quiet and wait."

Above them, heavy footsteps beat against the floor as a large group of men—"Soldiers," Petrad whispered—entered the house. There were shouts. Something hit the floor and crashed. They could hear the old woman, her voice squawking like a bird's, rebuke the men for barging in on her. Then the heavy footsteps came closer. They were right overhead, the voices now clearer. Someone said that an illegal meeting was taking place in her house. Did they see a meeting? she asked. Did they see anyone else there? The old woman demanded that they leave.

The men thumped and crashed around. Everyone watched the stairs to the secret hatchway, waiting to see if the soldiers would find it—and them. The tension was like a low hum in Maddy's ears.

"We should leave," one of the men suggested. "Quickly. Through the tunnel."

The rest agreed, and they moved to the far corner of the cellar. Petrad pulled a small chest away from the wall, revealing a square hole behind it. The women began going through, while the men looked at them and back at the stairwell anxiously.

Maddy hesitated where she was. "What about Annigua?" she asked.

"Yes," Simet said, also lingering, his eyes fixed on the stairs. "I don't like this."

Petrad returned and put his hands on their shoulders. "She'll be all right," he assured them.

But even before the words were out of his mouth, they heard the distinct sound of a slap, and Annigua cried out with pain. One of the soldiers shouted questions at her, demanding to know where the meeting was.

"They're roughing her up," Maddy stated, alarmed.

Simet rushed to the bottom of the stairs. Petrad followed, grabbing his arm. "Don't, Simet," he warned. "If you go up now, you'll be arrested, and then they'll have the evidence to convict her, you, and any of the rest of us they can catch. They'll also know about this secret room."

"I can't let them hurt her," he answered sternly.

"They won't do her much harm. You live in the palace, so you don't know what it's like for the rest of us. They'll knock her around, mess up her home, and then leave. But if you go up to help her ..."

Simet clenched his fists as he tried to decide. Then, angrily, he spun on his heels and went to the tunnel. The rest had already gone.

"We're going to leave her?" Maddy asked.

"We have to," Simet said sadly. Maddy thought she saw tears in his eyes, and then he ducked into the tunnel.

"Come along, child," Petrad whispered and nudged her along.

Maddy bit her lip. The last thing she heard as she entered the dark passage and Petrad pulled the chest back against the wall behind them was the sound of glass breaking and Annigua crying out a loud, "No!"

The tunnel led under several houses and emerged in a

stairwell, flooded from the day's rain, at the bottom of a large, industrial-looking building. The people went their separate ways without acknowledging one another. Simet and Maddy traveled in silence. Neither could escape the feeling that they'd abandoned poor Annigua.

To get back to the palace, they had to circle around to the street leading to Annigua's front door. As they walked, Maddy noticed a man in a long coat walking toward them. He looked at them, his eyes reflecting recognition, and then turned his face away ever so slightly. Maddy thought it was a curious action, but then she felt a twinge of recognition as well. She had seen the man somewhere before: the high forehead and heavyset eyes, the square jaw—at the palace, she was certain.

She intended to mention it to Simet, but they were now passing the small street leading to Annigua's house. Glancing in that direction, they could see the door standing open, a dim light coming from inside, the silhouette of someone moving about in the hall.

"It's no use," Simet groaned.

Maddy hated feeling so helpless. It seemed wrong to leave Annigua to the mercy of those terrible soldiers. Suddenly, without thinking, she turned and marched toward the door.

"What are you doing?" Simet asked, trailing her.

"Petrad didn't say we couldn't visit a friend, did he?"

Simet understood and nodded. Then, moving so quickly that Maddy almost didn't see him do it, he snatched up a handful of flowers from one of the boxes along the street. "Flowers for our friend," he explained.

They reached Annigua's door, a commotion of crashes and bangs still coming from inside. Simet pounded on the door and shouted out, "Hello? Are you at home, Annigua?"

A soldier appeared in the hallway. "What do you want?" he sneered at them.

"We have come to visit our friend." Simet held up the flowers as if to prove the statement. "Is there a problem here?"

"Your friend is busy," the soldier growled. "Come back tomorrow."

"But I'm very busy tomorrow. I must see her tonight."

The soldier approached them, eyeing them from head to foot as if to decide whether he could hurt them easily. "I said to go away!" He grabbed the edge of the door, intending to slam it in their faces, but Simet shoved his foot in the doorway. The soldier looked at him indignantly. "Do you want to be arrested?" he demanded.

"And do you want to explain to the king why you've arrested one of his palace guards?" Simet challenged.

The soldier was clearly surprised and took a second look at Simet. "What's that you say?" he asked.

Simet stepped into the door. "I am Simet, a palace guard for the king." He gestured to Maddy. "This is my protégée. Now, we've come to see our friend. And unless you can show me a warrant authorizing your insolence, we *will* see our friend."

Simet pushed the soldier aside and marched down the hallway. Maddy smiled at the guard, who stood with a numb expression on his face, and followed Simet.

The damage was worse than it had sounded. It looked as if they had literally turned the room upside down and shaken it until everything had either fallen or emptied. Three other soldiers stopped their destruction to look dumbfounded at Simet and Maddy.

Annigua sat like a crumpled doll in a chair off to the side. Her hand barely covered a red welt on her right cheek. Maddy's heart lurched at the sight. *It will be a deep black and blue in no time at all,* Maddy thought.

"Annigua?" Simet said.

Annigua looked up, her face alight with the surprise of seeing him. Her eyes quickly went to the rug and the trapdoor as if he'd come up through it and she had somehow missed the moment.

"We brought you flowers," Maddy said brightly. Simet gave them to her. She took them uneasily, as if she still couldn't figure out what had happened.

"We were passing by and thought we'd stop in to visit you," Simet explained. "But I see you have visitors. What goes on?"

"They're ruining my house!" the old woman sobbed, tears filling her eyes. "They're accusing me of things! What's our nation coming to when barbarians can invade an old woman's home like this?"

"That's a question I would like answered, too," Simet said, scowling at the soldiers.

The soldier who had met them at the door entered the room. He seemed to have gotten over his shock. "Look, you two, we're here on the business of Lord Hector," he declared. "And if you don't leave right this minute, I *will* arrest you for obstructing justice."

"Then you'll have to arrest us," Simet challenged. "And let the consequences fall heavily upon your shoulders."

The soldier looked at Simet for a moment. Then he shrugged and barked at his companions, "Take them to Lord Hector."

CHAPTER EIGHT

※————※

"Well, well," Lord Hector said disapprovingly a short while later. He stood next to a large bookcase in his office, as if posing for a portrait. He lightly fingered one of the books. "What am I to make of this?"

"Make whatever you like of it," Simet replied. His eyes were cold, his jaw set as he dropped himself into a chair across from Lord Hector's desk. Maddy had never seen him look so angry. She sat down in another chair nearby.

"I can't help but wonder why you two were visiting a known criminal," he said in a voice of satin. "Come to think of it, I can't help but wonder why you two were together at all. Are you friends?"

"We have mutual friends," Simet answered. "Annigua is one of them. And she is *not* a criminal."

"So *you* say." Lord Hector clasped his hands behind his back and sauntered to his desk with a forced casualness. "I happen to know she is a fanatic of the Old Faith, an illegal cult. I also happen to know that she conducts secret meetings in her house. Quite a coincidence that you were there tonight."

"No one has yet said that visiting a friend whenever I like is a crime."

Lord Hector smiled. "You should choose your friends more wisely."

"Are you now determining who can and cannot be friends in Marus?"

"In the interests of the king, I may well determine *a lot* of things, including that," Lord Hector sneered. "You know that believing in the Old Faith is contrary to the king's wishes, and I am determined to eliminate that faith. Even tonight, my soldiers are paying surprise visits on suspected members."

"Visits—or attacks?" Simet asked.

"That depends on whether they resist."

"Annigua didn't resist," Maddy suddenly said, "and your soldiers still beat her up."

"Oh?" Lord Hector countered. "Were you there when it happened? How do you know whether she resisted? Is that what she told you, or are you going by some other source of information?"

Maddy pressed her lips together and lowered her head. She was afraid that if she said any more, she might reveal that she *had* been there.

Then a question came to Maddy's mind. Did Lord Hector already know that? Was it possible that she and Simet had been followed to Annigua's house? Maddy remembered the man she'd seen in the street. Was he one of Lord Hector's spies? If so, Lord Hector knew full well that they were there. He might even have sent his soldiers in to catch them in the act. If that were the case, he was merely toying with them now. *Can he do anything to us without proof?* she wondered.

"I'll allow that you happened to be in the wrong place at the wrong time," Lord Hector offered, as if pardoning them. "But there are other matters on my mind. Your oath of allegiance, Simet—I want it on my desk in the morning."

"You will not have it," Simet replied.

Lord Hector's face went red. "What?" he sputtered. "Do you openly defy me?"

Simet stood up. "I appeal to the king."

"You can't."

"As a member of his royal guards, I have the right to

appeal anything you or any of his other officials decree. So I appeal."

"Why will you not sign an oath of allegiance unless you're not loyal to the king? Or perhaps you really are one of those fanatics of the Old Faith?"

"I am a Marutian and bound by no Palatian oath of allegiance. I will appeal to the king on that basis. Even *he* respects the differences between our two nations, united or not."

"He is king over all, which means you are bound by his laws!" Lord Hector nearly shouted.

"Then I will wait to hear him declare that for himself," Simet said calmly. "Until that time, I will remain under our Marutian law, which says that no Marutian in a royal position can sign an oath of allegiance to any other government."

Lord Hector grunted. "You quibble over technicalities."

"If necessary. But you can do nothing to me until he returns from his honeymoon to settle the matter."

Lord Hector narrowed his weasellike eyes until they were mere slits. "We'll see about that," he threatened. He walked over to a window and pulled the curtain aside. "By the way, tonight I issued a new decree. We'll call it *Lord Hector's Decree*."

"How original."

"It says that to follow or subscribe to the Old Faith is now punishable by death." He let the significance of his announcement settle into Simet and Maddy's minds. "And in anticipation of the great number of superstitious fools my soldiers will catch, you see"—he nodded toward the window—"I have begun the construction of a new gallows." Lord Hector smiled devilishly. "It's been specially designed for them. They will be allowed to *kneel* before they're hung."

"No!" Simet said in an appalled whisper.

Lord Hector turned to him. "As a member of the palace

guard, you may have the right to appeal to the king, but the rest of your countrymen do not. They are average citizens who must enjoy the justice of *my* courts. Now get out! I have work to do."

Simet glared at Lord Hector, then turned to leave. Maddy stood up, but Hector suddenly added, "No, I want the girl to stay for a moment."

Maddy looked at Simet, worry in her eyes. He nodded at her as if to say, "Be brave." He walked out and closed the door behind him.

Lord Hector sat down in the chair behind his desk and gazed at Maddy. "You, dear girl, are a puzzle to me. My people can find out nearly anything I want to know about anyone, but you don't seem to have a history. You might have fallen from one of the two moons for all I know."

Maddy didn't respond.

"Because you seem to be a favorite with our new queen, I want to give you the benefit of the doubt. I want to believe you're merely young and impressionable and have slipped under the misguided influence of Simet."

He waited a moment to see if she would now speak. She didn't.

"Do you understand what's happening in this kingdom? It isn't a conflict between Palatia and Marus. It's not a battle over geography or heritage. It's a battle over *ideas*. The *new* ideas of Palatia are those of a world made better by the supremacy of mankind. We reject the *old* ideas of those few fools who still believe in unseen gods, who have faith in things outside our control."

Maddy watched him silently.

He rested his elbows on his desk and folded his hands in front of him. "You seem to be a perceptive girl. Surely you must see where—and with whom—the future lies. Join the winning side. Use those sharp eyes and ears of yours for those who will benefit you the most. Put them to use for your king and beloved queen. Work with me and help me to root out the believers in the Old Faith. It will put you in good standing with our monarchs." He paused again. "Well?"

Maddy wanted to say a resounding *no* right away, but she thought better of offending him. Simet could appeal to the king, but could she? Would her ties to Annison be enough to protect her?

"An answer, if you please," Lord Hector persisted.

Maddy cleared her throat nervously and spoke as diplomatically as she could. "I would like to speak to Queen Annison about it, to seek her advice," she declared.

Lord Hector's expression, which had been alive from his anticipation of her answer, now fell back to its normal boredom. "If you insist," he said coldly.

"I wouldn't dare do anything without her permission," Maddy explained and stood up.

LordHector leaned back in his chair. "In the meantime, you had better be careful, child. Anything can happen to you in a large palace like this. People can disappear and not be missed for days."

Maddy didn't reply but left the room as quickly as she could.

Maddy was awakened the next morning by Tabby's loud voice. She sounded agitated as she spoke with one of the other servants.

"Riots!" she said. "It's as if the people have lost their minds!

They're in the streets, fighting the king's soldiers, tearing the city apart!"

Maddy got out of bed, wrapped her robe around her, and went into the main chamber. Tabby stood in the center of the room, gesturing wildly as she spoke.

"It's all because of Lord Hector's decree. He's going to *execute* anyone associated with the Old Faith. Mind you, I couldn't care less about superstitions like that, but I hate to see Marutians slaughtered for such an absurd reason. I wonder if the king knows? I wonder if anyone has told Annison? It's an outrage, that's what it is. An outrage!"

"The believers in the Old Faith are rioting?" the servant girl asked in a shrill voice.

"Maybe some of them, I don't know. But the decree has brought *all* Marutians into the streets. Don't you see? They're rioting because the decree violates their civil liberties. They say this is the first step to complete domination."

The servant girl clutched her apron and strangled it nervously. "What will happen to us? Do you think the mobs will win against the soldiers?"

"Anything is possible."

Maddy leaned against the doorway, trying to take it all in. Was this the rebellion that might overthrow King Willem's forces in Marus? Was it possible that Annison hadn't needed to marry the king after all?

Maddy spent the day going about her duties—more packing for the queen—but kept her ears open for news about the riots. Occasionally, through the open glass doors, she could hear a distant roar of people, then muskets being fired, but the palace seemed like a remote island otherwise. At midday, she heard a rumor that Lord Hector had several regiments positioned around the palace to make certain it was safe.

Deep in her memory, she recalled the stories from her grandparents about how the Russian revolutionaries stormed the cities, vandalizing homes and palaces, driving those who resisted into the streets. Some members of her family had crowded into a church for sanctuary, only to have the church burned down around them. Several had died.

Now she was on the other side. She *wanted* the Marutians to win. She wanted the mobs to force the Palatians out of the country so they could believe and worship freely again. But could they do it? How could a disorganized mob fight against a powerful army?

Maddy also wondered about Simet. Would he take to the streets to help the mob, or would he stay to protect the palace? Where was his allegiance at a time like this?

As midday turned into afternoon and afternoon turned into evening, Maddy decided to go to the bell tower at six to see if Simet was there. She crept cautiously along the halls, even going the wrong way several times to make sure she wasn't being followed. Though it was a period of crisis, she didn't doubt that Lord Hector might have someone keeping an eye on her. But it seemed as if all the men were out of the palace, and the few maids and servant girls she saw didn't seem to pay her any attention.

The old, wooden door to the bell tower was already ajar when Maddy reached it. Normally it was closed and locked unless Simet was already there, in which case he would open the door as she approached. They then met either in the doorway or, if they were worried about being seen, just inside the tower, at the base of the stone steps that curled up to the top.

Maddy peeked her head through the open door. "Simet?" she whispered.

No one answered.

She thought about turning around and going back to Annison's chambers, but it occurred to her that she'd never been to the top of the tower. Her meetings with Simet had always been so rushed that she hadn't asked him to let her see what it was like. Glancing around quickly, she closed the door. A pale light spread down like a fan from somewhere above. She went to the stone steps and began her ascent.

She had no idea how high the tower went, and she lost count of the steps somewhere around 100. They continued to circle upward, and she was now determined to make it to the top. She hoped Simet was up there somewhere.

Then she wondered what she would do if Simet *wasn't* up above. Perhaps no one was there and the door had been left ajar by accident. Or, worse, what if Lord Hector were there? How would she explain her presence in the tower? But her aching legs told her it was too much of a waste to go back now. So she persevered.

Eventually she reached another wooden door, similar to the one at the bottom. It, too, was slightly ajar. As quietly as possible, she pushed it open and stepped out onto the belfry. It was enclosed on four sides by walls nearly as tall as Maddy and pillars that reached up to the bell encasement. She looked up, expecting to see a large bell, but it had been removed. Pigeons' nests now littered the wooden slats where a bell had once hung.

A man stood at the opposite end of the belfry, gazing out at Sarum. Without seeing the face, Maddy knew who it was.

"Simet?" she said softly.

He didn't turn but responded, "Do you see?"

Maddy could. The view was breathtaking. Tall, monumental buildings rose up amidst smaller roofs. Towers reached upward like large pencils. The streets and avenues, obviously based on old horse paths rather than planned roads, criss-crossed like a spider's web. In the distance was a large bridge that stretched over a river. It was a magnificent sight.

There was more to see than just a view of a beautiful city, however. Billows of smoke rose up like black cotton over whole sections. Every now and then she thought she heard the pop of a gun, and then she realized it was a cannon. Buildings in some sections of the city lay in ruins.

"It's more than I can bear," Simet groaned. Only then did Maddy realize he was weeping. "The Palatian army has broken up the mob. Most of the fighting has stopped. Lord Hector has won."

"What will happen now?"

"Lord Hector will come down like an iron fist on the dis-senters. He will execute those who actively fought against him and then resume his persecution of the Old Faith."

Maddy felt heartsick at the news. Things could only get worse now.

"Oh, who will come and save us?" Simet implored, and then Maddy realized he was praying out loud. "Who will be our deliverer? Send us an intercessor. Otherwise, the night will fall and we will never see the day again." He bowed his head and wept uncontrollably over the city.

Maddy put her arm around his waist, and he pulled her close. Tears formed in her eyes, and she found herself praying along with him. "Help us," she whispered. "Send us a deliverer."

CHAPTER NINE

S imet was right. Lord Hector fell on Marus like an iron fist. The jails and dungeons were filled with many of the rioters, and his soldiers raided the homes of anyone suspected of being involved with the Old Faith.

Just as disturbing was the effectiveness of a special group of secret police Lord Hector had created. They worked diligently to spread propaganda that the members of the Old Faith had started the riots that nearly destroyed the city. They claimed that Lord Hector had uncovered a plot in which the members of the Old Faith planned to kill Queen Annison when she returned from her honeymoon. Then the secret police not only spied on the people of Sarum, but they also encouraged the people to spy on one another. Soon neighbor turned against neighbor, reporting suspicious activities or offhand statements that sounded treasonous. Petrad was betrayed by a neighbor and arrested.

Maddy heard all this through Simet as they continued to meet every other day. She worried about Simet. As time passed, he began to look worn out. He seemed to be aging right before her very eyes.

"Lord Hector is winning," he said to her in their latest conversation, his voice old and tired. "In only three weeks, he has brought us to the edge of destruction. I don't know how many of us will be left by the time Annison returns."

"But Lord Hector hasn't executed anyone," Maddy reminded him. "He's waiting for the king to come back. You said so yourself. He wants to hand them over like trophies, just to show what a good job he's doing."

"But how many will be left by the time the king gets here?" Simet asked. "He tortures them daily. I have no doubt the weak among them will succumb to disease, if not starvation, around the time the king returns. Lord Hector will kill them off before they can be formally executed."

After a moment of silence, Simet confessed, "I went back to Annigua's house the other night. It's been boarded up. I learned from a neighbor that she was arrested and locked in the dungeon. After only a week, she died."

Together Maddy and Simet prayed. Then Simet said quietly, "I've come to realize that Annison may be our only hope. She must persuade the king somehow to reverse what Lord Hector has done."

Meanwhile, Lord Hector was unrelenting. On the eve of King Willem and Queen Annison's return, he called the entire palace staff, including Annison's court, to the Great Hall. He stood before them dressed in his usual black coat, with the usual leer on his face. Many of his soldiers and secret police stood behind him on the stage. One of them was the man with the high forehead that Maddy had seen in the street outside Annigua's house that night of the meeting. Maddy knew then that he'd been following either her or Simet. The thought sent a chill up and down her spine. How often had she been watched or followed without her realizing it?

"I have an announcement," Lord Hector declared. "Tomorrow, when the king and queen return, I will inform them that I want to celebrate their new reign in Sarum with a cleansing of the kingdom. We're going to scrub out the old ideas, the old ways, the old faith once and for all. We will have a final *purge* of those who resist the new ideas, the new ways, and the new faith in the supremacy of our king!"

Some of the Palatians in the crowd cheered. The rest listened in stunned silence. Maddy felt her heart drop to her feet.

Lord Hector continued, "I want the entire city—no, the entire *nation*—to join in as we dig up the last of the weeds in our beautiful garden. What better way to present the kingdom to His Majesty!"

The Palatians applauded, many of them nudging the rest of the crowd to join in. Soon the room was a roar of applause. Maddy kept her hands at her side. Giving her a sharp elbow in the side, Tabby whispered, "Even if you don't agree, applaud. People are looking."

Maddy didn't care and stubbornly kept her fists clenched. She thought only about that phrase "a final purge." She imagined the frenzied soldiers riding through the streets, trampling or bayoneting their suspects; the mobs of sympathizers setting fire to the homes and buildings that were suspected havens of the Old Faith; and innocent people being dragged out and beaten, probably killed, by anyone with a desire to do so.

She looked around the room for Simet but couldn't see him anywhere. What was his reaction to the news? Maddy then saw him standing near the doors. He was stone-faced, his expression empty, betraying nothing. She wanted to go to him, to find out what he thought they should do. But she knew that Lord Hector or one of his men would be watching.

Their eyes caught each other. Maddy wanted to see some sense of hope in his expression. But he simply shook his head and walked out.

The despair in his expression filled her with dread.

King Willem and Queen Annison arrived at the palace early the next afternoon. Protocol demanded that the staff line up in the front hall to present themselves to the returning couple. They applauded as the king and queen stepped through the front doors.

King Willem took a dramatic bow. He looked happy and rested. He had begun to grow a beard and mustache while he was away, which made him look more mature. And he had gotten rid of his wild wigs and now let his own hair be seen. He looked like a proper king, Maddy thought.

Queen Annison looked as beautiful as ever. Her raven hair was longer and pulled back in an unfamiliar style. "She's been to one of those awful Palatian hairdressers," Tabby whispered to Maddy. "We'll put that right in no time."

Apart from that, nothing about Annison's appearance made Maddy think anything had changed. She had the same gentle smile, and her eyes reflected an inner resolve, a strength, that comforted Maddy.

"Do you think she knows what's been happening here?" Maddy asked Tabby.

Tabby shook her head. "Probably not," she replied. "The king wouldn't think it's a woman's place to know or care about the affairs of government. In fact, I wouldn't be a bit surprised if Lord Hector kept even the king in the dark about what he's been doing. But the king will find out soon enough."

Maddy stood by, barely maintaining her patience, while Tabby gave Annison a tour of her new chambers.

"They're larger than the others," Annison said, pleased. She went out to the balcony, which was smaller than the balcony in the other section of the palace. "And I believe I like the view of these gardens better than our other view."

Maddy realized that even if Annison hated the new chambers, she was too kind to have said so.

"Tabby, please be sure to thank everyone for their hard

work in moving all my things so efficiently," Annison instructed.

"Of course, my queen."

Annison giggled. "Don't be silly," she chided gently. "When we're in these chambers, I am, and always will be, Annison. You may save the formalities of calling me *queen* for the formal places."

Tabby bowed slightly. "Yes, Your Highness."

Annison laughed and waved her away. "Leave me with Maddy for a few moments."

Tabby frowned. "I think you'd be wise to allow me to inform you about—"

"No, Tabby. I want to speak with Maddy first, and then you can tell me all the latest news and gossip."

"As you wish," Tabby said unhappily and retreated from the room.

Annison sat on the edge of her bed and patted a spot next to her. "Come, Maddy. Sit down and tell me everything. Is Simet well? When can we exchange messages again?"

Maddy didn't sit down but stayed where she was near the window. She opened her mouth to speak but suddenly felt a ball of tears rise in her throat. She swallowed hard to make it go away.

A shadow crossed Annison's face. "Maddy, what's wrong?"

"You were gone such a long time" was all that Maddy could say.

"We were at the king's cottage in the southern mountains of Palatia," Annison explained. "The king received regular reports from one of his servants, but he never shared them with me. Has something happened? Is Simet all right?"

Maddy went to the bed and sat down next to the queen. She couldn't look Annison in the eyes and lowered her head.

Annison touched her face, lifting her chin with a gentle hand. "Tell me what's wrong, Maddy."

Then, like a dam bursting, the words came—as did the tears—and Maddy told Annison everything that had happened after she left for her honeymoon.

Annison's face went pale as Maddy spoke, but she struggled to keep her composure. Agitated, she then stood up and paced, wringing her hands, her eyes darting back and forth as her mind tried to work through the terrible news.

"Where is Simet now?" she asked once Maddy had finished.

"I don't know. But one of the last things he said to me was that you are the only hope. You must persuade the king to undo what Lord Hector is doing."

"Me?" Annison paused again to think. Then she returned to the bed, sat down, and took one of Maddy's hands in hers. Her voice shook as she spoke. "Listen to me, Maddy. Now is not the time for tears. We'll weep together later. Right now we must do something to avert this horrible plan."

"Do what?" Maddy asked helplessly.

"I need more information ..." Annison's sentence trailed off as an idea came to her. "The passageway."

"Passageway?"

"Yes. If you go to the king's reception room now, you may hear what Lord Hector is reporting to him."

"There's a passageway from these chambers?"

"Yes." Annison was on her feet again. She went around the bed to the side nearest the wall. In the corner, she felt along the edge of one of the panels, then pressed her hand down. The edge gave way, and the panel sprung open.

"But I don't know the way," Maddy complained.

Annison held up her hand and went to a small end table. She picked up a piece of paper and a pen and quickly scribbled the directions. "This will take you to the same main passage-way where you were before. You'll remember it." Annison thrust the paper into Maddy's hand and guided her to the entrance. She reached up into the passageway and retrieved a torch. After lighting it, she gave it to Maddy and sent her on her way.

Annison had moved so decisively that Maddy didn't have time to think about what had happened in the passageway with Lord Hector. But the memory returned as she crept through the dark shadows. In a few minutes, she reached the peephole she had used to watch Hector and the king before. She slid the cover back and peeked through. The king, dressed in lime green, was sitting on his throne, looking bored as usual. And Lord Hector, in his black coat, stood in front of him, his hands clasped behind his back. He was talking about the finances of the region and how much money was in the king's treasury. This went on for a few minutes.

Finally the king said, "I've heard enough about money and economics, Hector. I want to hear what you've been doing to this city while I was gone."

Lord Hector smiled. "Of course, Your Majesty," he replied. "I was saving the best for last."

The king frowned. "I was greatly troubled by the reports of riots."

"No more than I was when they happened, sire," Hector said innocently. "But I've learned that they were incited by members of your nemesis, the Old Faith, and I've been work-ing with particular diligence to capture them."

The king rested his chin on his hand. "Tell me everything."

With great embellishment, Lord Hector told the king how he had sent his soldiers to suspected meeting houses to break up illegal worship services. He claimed that many of the members actively resisted the soldiers, even resorting to violence, whereupon his men had to use greater force. "A few of the culprits died before we could bring them to justice," he said, as if saddened by their deaths. "One or two of our soldiers were scratched and bruised."

Maddy was astounded by the unflinching way Hector lied. She wanted to scream at him from where she was but resisted the temptation.

"As a result," Lord Hector continued, "I issued a decree forbidding the Old Faith in your kingdom and stepped up our efforts to rid the land of the vermin. They retaliated by causing riots among the gentler and good citizens of Sarum."

The king scratched his chin. "It still puzzles me. I was certain the believers in the Old Faith were against violence."

"As I've told you, Your Majesty, they seem peaceful enough until threatened. And then they come roaring forth like lions."

"So where is all this leading to?" the king asked impatiently. "I have a game of golf to play this afternoon."

"I'm pleased to say that I have diminished the threat to you by the members of the Old Faith. I believe we have captured most of the ringleaders and destroyed their meeting places."

"Then the crisis is over," the king said as if concluding the discussion.

"Not quite," Lord Hector replied. "I'm calling on all law-abiding and peaceful people in the nation to engage in one final purge to rid the kingdom of this infestation—as a celebration of your return from your honeymoon."

"Meaning what?"

"Meaning that this coming Saturday, all good Palatians and Marutians who are loyal to Your Majesty will drive the Old Faith out once and for all. Then I will empty the dungeons and jails of the traitors and execute them, according to Your Majesty's pleasure."

"Yes, I noticed the new scaffolds you were building," the king said in a doubtful tone. "Are you sure the Marutians are behind this idea of yours? I wouldn't want them to get upset and revolt or anything like that."

"The Marutians are as tired of the Old Faith as we are, Your Majesty. They welcome our efforts to get rid of it. Like us, they wish to turn their faces toward the bright sun of your new and enlightened ideas."

The king rubbed his hands together as if to end the meeting. "Good. Well done. Let me know how it all turns out."

That's that, Maddy thought with a sense of defeat. *The king has approved the purge.*

Lord Hector cleared his throat before the king could get to his feet. "There is one other matter, sire."

"What?" the king asked, annoyed.

"One of your palace guards ..."

"A guard? What about him?"

"Well, I have tried repeatedly and in a reasonable manner to get him to sign the oath of allegiance to Your Majesty. And now," Lord Hector said with a chuckle, "he insists on appealing to you rather than signing the oath."

"Appeal to me?"

"Apparently it's his right as a palace guard to appeal directly to the king," Lord Hector replied, then added offhandedly, "It's one of those Marutian laws I want to change as soon as we can."

"I see. Well, what about it?"

"I have evidence—not cold, hard evidence, mind you— but evidence nonetheless that this particular guard won't sign because he is a fanatic of the Old Faith."

"Why are you telling me about this?" The king now stood up. "Why haven't you locked him up and interrogated him?"

"As I said, he appealed to you, and I can't touch him without your permission."

"Then consider his appeal heard and denied. I can't be bothered with this nonsense." Without saying anything else, the king stepped down from the throne and left the room.

"Of course, Your Majesty," Lord Hector said to the empty room.

Maddy wasted no time rushing back to Annison's chambers. After emerging in the bedroom, she burst in on Annison in a side room that served as a reception room. Annison was listening intently to Tabby.

Tabby glowered at Maddy, displeased by the rudeness of the interruption.

"I'm sorry, Your Highness," Maddy said breathlessly, "but I have news."

"Leave us, Tabby," Annison commanded.

"But Your Highness—"

Annison gave Tabby an uncharacteristically stern look. Tabby stood up, bowed, and left the room, nearly slamming the door behind her.

Maddy reported what she'd seen and heard in the king's reception room. Annison's eyes went wide, and she reached out to take Maddy's hand. "You have to run and warn Simet," she urged. "Tell him to escape and hide until it's safe again. Go, dear girl, *go!*"

Maddy left in a flash and hurried down the many hallways of the palace. She had no fear of becoming lost now; she was getting to know her way around pretty well. She got to Simet's small office just as he was coming out.

"Simet!" she gasped.

He was surprised to see her. "Hello, child," he greeted. "Your timing is perfect. I am about to seek an audience with the king to discuss my appeal—and to tell him all the terrible things his chancellor has been doing."

"Lord Hector ... has beaten you to it," Maddy said in heaving tones. "The king has given him permission for the purge ... *and* to arrest you. Annison wants you to escape. You have to hurry!"

Simet looked bewildered, as if Maddy had suddenly walked up and hit him in the face with a rock. "This can't be," he said in a half whisper, then cried out, "Where is justice? Where is the Unseen One?"

"He's only in your imagination," Lord Hector said as he approached from the end of the hall. "It's where He's always been. But thank you for confirming what I always suspected, that you're one of the fanatics of the Old Faith."

"Run, Simet!" Maddy implored. "Run!"

But it was too late. Lord Hector's guards swarmed around them like bees and grabbed Simet by both arms.

One of them, the man with the high forehead, punched Simet in the mouth. "That's for making my job so difficult," he spat.

Simet shook his head as if shaking off the blow, but a trickle of blood slipped from his lip.

Maddy gave the man a hard kick in his shin.

He winced and then suddenly laughed at her. "You're a feisty one," he observed. "I've enjoyed watching you."

Lord Hector stepped in between Maddy and the man. "Take Simet to my *special* interrogation room in the dungeon," he commanded.

Simet said nothing as the guards took him away.

Lord Hector grabbed Maddy roughly by the arm. "I warned

you to choose your side carefully," he said coldly.

Maddy looked at him defiantly. "I am on the *queen's* side," she challenged. "Are you going to arrest me, too?"

Lord Hector grunted and let go of her. "You'd be advised to stay very close to the queen, then. And stay clear of anything to do with Simet. He's as good as dead."

CHAPTER TEN

❦ ———————— ❦

"What are we to do?" Annison asked over and over as she paced from one end of her bedroom to another.

Maddy watched her go back and forth. "Can't you talk to the king like Simet said?" she asked. "You're his wife, after all."

Annison shook her head. "It isn't that easy. According to Palatian law, the queen can only be summoned by the king. She can never approach him on her own initiative."

"What happens if you break their law?"

"He could divorce me or, worse, have me arrested and put to death."

"That sounds like a stupid law."

Annison agreed and then worried aloud, "He warned me when we returned that he would be very busy this week. I don't think he planned to see me again until next week sometime—*after* Hector's purge. And after Simet has been murdered."

"What if you bumped into him by accident?" Maddy suggested. "What if you just happened to be somewhere that *he* happened to be?"

Annison considered the idea for a moment, then commented, "I don't know of any Palatian laws against that."

"Then you could talk to the king and make him understand."

"But that's another question," Annison said thoughtfully. Tired of pacing, she sat down in a chair. "What can I say to make him understand? He doesn't believe women should be involved in affairs of state to begin with. Worse, if I appeal to him on behalf of the Old Faith, he'll wonder why I'm doing it. That would leave me with only one choice: to tell him the truth."

"The truth?" Maddy asked. "The *whole* truth?"

"Yes. I'll have to confess that I myself am a believer and that Simet has been like a father to me."

"What do you think he'll do if you say all that?"

"I don't know." Annison contemplated the consequences. "He might very well feel betrayed and allow Lord Hector to kill me along with all the others."

"Then maybe you shouldn't do it. Maybe there's another way."

"What other way, Maddy? You've been sent here by the Unseen One to be my helper. Now *help* me. Tell me of another way to save my people and I'll do it. Otherwise, don't distract me from what I know, and you know, I must do."

Properly chastised, Maddy fell silent. Her mind went back to when she'd first arrived in Marus with her fairy-tale hopes and storybook dreams and hadn't understood Annison's commitment to duty. Then it was the duty of marrying a man she didn't love. Now Maddy realized that marrying the king was only a small thing to do. Her real duty for the Unseen One meant that she might have to give her life to save the people she loved.

Annison gazed at Maddy as if she knew her thoughts. "You see now, don't you?" she quizzed. "What good is our faith in anything if we're not willing to sacrifice ourselves to it completely—even die for it?"

Maddy nodded and made up her mind. If Annison were going to sacrifice, she would sacrifice, too.

Annison looked at the clock on the mantle. "If the king is golfing this afternoon, he'll return to his chambers around five o'clock. That gives me a few hours to prepare. Come help me get dressed."

Maddy looked at her questioningly.

"If I'm going to bump into the king, I want to look presentable," she explained with a smile.

As she dressed, Annison decided that her panic about Simet and Hector's purge mustn't rule her thinking. If she had to appeal to the king, she needed to do so in a subtle and intelligent manner.

"I must learn from Lord Hector," she told Maddy. "I must have a plan even more clever than his own. Then I must speak to the king as Lord Hector does."

"You mean lie?" Maddy asked.

"Of course not!" Annison replied. "But there are more ways to appeal to the king than simply throwing oneself at his feet or confronting him with our cause. We must get him in the right frame of mind to consider other notions before we make our case."

Maddy was impressed with Annison's calm and collected manner. Maddy, on the other hand, was a bundle of nerves. All the subtlety and cleverness in the world wouldn't make a difference if the king rejected Annison and her faith.

Annison went to her desk and pulled out a small, red book. She sat down and began to write in it. After a moment, she seemed self-conscious about Maddy's standing nearby and dismissed her. Maddy waited in the other room, wondering what Annison was up to.

It was close to 4:30 when Annison came out of her room. "Tabby has learned from one of the king's servants that he'll return from his golf game through one of the entrances in the east garden," she told Maddy. "I'll make it a point to be strolling in that garden when he arrives."

"I'll be with you," Maddy said.

"No, you won't," Annison stated firmly. "This is dangerous. If it all goes wrong, you must leave the palace immediately. One way or another, you must find your way home."

Maddy was distressed. "Home? How am I supposed to go home? I don't know how I got here in the first place!"

"Then we'll hope and pray that the Unseen One will send you back if our plans are undone."

"But I want to go with you," Maddy pouted.

"No. You wait here." Annison clutched the small, red book against her chest. She then adjusted her shawl, gathered up her dress, and strolled casually out of the room. For a fraction of a second, it was easy to think she was merely a woman going for a walk in a garden—and not to her possible doom.

Maddy lasted all of five minutes in the room alone. Then her eye caught an umbrella leaning against the wall, and she decided Annison would need it to shield her from the sun or protect her from the rain, if it happened to fall. It seemed like a good excuse either way, so she grabbed it and headed for the east garden.

It was a beautiful summer's day, and the sun poured golden rays down to highlight the lush greens, blues, purples, yellows, and reds of the garden. Maddy looked around for Annison but couldn't see her. Suddenly a hand was on her arm.

"What are you doing here?" Annison asked as Maddy turned to face her.

Maddy smiled up at her and said feebly, "I brought you this umbrella."

Annison wagged a finger at her. "You've disobeyed me," she stated. "Now go back to my chambers."

Maddy opened her mouth to argue, but the sound of an approaching coach stopped her. It was the king's coach, coming up a gravel path that traveled along one side of the garden. The driver drew the horses to a halt only feet away from where Annison and Maddy stood. The door swung open and the king stepped out.

"Hello, my dear," he said pleasantly as soon as he saw the queen. "What a nice surprise!"

Annison bowed to him and nudged Maddy to do the same. "Thank you, my king," Annison replied. "I've been enjoying the garden."

"May I walk with you for a moment?" the king asked, blushing a little like a schoolboy.

"I would be honored."

The king took the queen's arm in his, and they strolled toward the large fountain that stood at the center of the garden. Maddy followed at a discreet distance, but she could hear what they were saying.

The king initially dominated the conversation with talk about his golf game. Then, when it was clear they had exhausted that topic, Annison said, "My lord, I know you're terribly busy now that we've returned. But I would like to ask a favor . . ."

"A favor, my queen? Name it and it's yours, even up to half my kingdom," he said playfully.

"I would be grateful if you and Lord Hector would come to lunch in my chambers tomorrow."

"We would be delighted!" the king replied, then added sourly, "But do I have to bring Hector? He's been getting on my nerves lately."

"As your queen, I think it would be wise for me to be in good standing with your chancellor. Don't you think?"

"You are diplomatic as well as beautiful!" the king exclaimed. He kissed her hand. "I am to meet Hector in a few moments and will present your invitation."

"Thank you, sire. It will be a modest meal, but I treasure any time we have together."

The king blushed again, then stroked his growing beard with the back of his hand. "You are a joy to me, Annison. I will see you at lunchtime tomorrow."

"Until then," Annison said, and she handed him the book she was carrying. It was covered in red velvet and had a small, gold clasp along the front. It was the one Maddy had seen her writing in earlier. "This is a small gift from me in the meantime. It's a story I wrote for you. But you mustn't read it until later."

"I'm intrigued," the king said and took the book gratefully. He kissed Annison's hand again. "Thank you." With only a passing glance toward Maddy, he walked to the back door of the palace, whistling a jaunty tune.

Once the king was out of earshot, Annison took Maddy aside. "You must be quick now," she instructed. "I want you to go back down the passage to hear what's said between the king and Lord Hector. Hurry now!"

Maddy found most of the conversation between the king and Lord Hector boring. They discussed more financial details, legislation about Palatians living in Marutian homes, the positioning of troops, and a series of meetings the king was to have with local businessmen. The king hardly seemed interested.

Then, when the meeting was drawing to a close, the king said, "My Lord Hector, I hope you don't have any plans for lunch tomorrow."

" I don't, sire," Lord Hector replied. "Why do you ask?"

"The queen has invited us to lunch in her chambers."

"Us? The two of us?"

"Yes. She asked for you specifically."

"Well, I'm honored, Your Majesty. I wouldn't miss it."

"And so you shouldn't."

The king left the reception room by way of a back door, and Maddy nearly closed the peephole to return to Annison. But Lord Hector did a curious thing. He suddenly marched up to the throne and sat down on it, slinging his leg over one of the chair arms.

"Well, well," he said aloud.

The man with the high forehead came forward from the door. Maddy wasn't sure if he'd been there the whole time and she just hadn't noticed him, or if he'd only just entered. "You look rather pleased with yourself," he observed.

"Why shouldn't I be, Reginald?" Lord Hector responded. "Things are looking up."

"Are you talking about the purge or the king's golf score?"

"I'm talking about being invited to the queen's chambers for lunch tomorrow. What do you make of it?"

Reginald shrugged. "I'm not sure I make anything of it."

"But why invite *me* when she could have the king all to herself?"

"A very good question. I suppose you think you have an answer?"

"I do. I believe it's a gesture on her part to win my friend-ship. I think she's a very shrewd woman, and she knows where the real power in this kingdom rests. With me. She also knows that now is a very good time to win my favor."

"You read a lot into a simple invitation."

"In the business of politics, one has to. Nothing is as it seems. No one is kind unless they will gain from it. No one is nasty unless there's an advantage. That's how the game is played."

"But she's only the queen," Reginald said. "She has no real power."

"It's true," Lord Hector conceded. "But she's a beautiful woman."

"You've said yourself that she seems rather simpleminded. Why would you bother with a simpleminded woman?"

"Because I believe she has the king's heart." Hector sat up, abruptly changing the subject. "Tell me how Simet is holding up. Has he given you any worthwhile information? It would be gratifying to me if he would blab the names of all the other leaders of the Old Faith."

"No, sir. He defies us at every turn. He has surprising stamina for an old man."

"You won't kill him."

"Of course not. I leave that pleasure to you on Saturday."

Hector chuckled low and wickedly. "He will be the first to die on my new gallows." Hector then stood up, his tone turning light. "I wonder what I should wear to the queen's chambers tomorrow?"

"Your black coat, I assume."

"Yes," Hector said thoughtfully. "It's my favorite."

Maddy finally went back to Annison's chambers. Annison was in the midst of finalizing the menu for the next day's lunch with the king. Tabby took copious notes, offering suggestions on one or two items, and then hustled off to inform the royal chef.

"What did you learn?" Annison asked Maddy once they were alone.

"Lord Hector thinks you've invited him to lunch because you want to be his friend," Maddy replied. "And they're trying to get Simet to give them the names of the leaders of the Old Faith."

"They're torturing him," said Annison softly.

Maddy nodded somberly. "But he hasn't told them anything."

"And he won't. He'll die first."

"They won't let him die," Maddy said. "Lord Hector wants Simet to be the first one hung on the gallows this Saturday."

Annison clutched her hands to her breast. "If the Unseen One would permit it, I would poison that evil man's food tomorrow. But that's not His way. It's not what I believe I should do."

"What *are* you going to do?" Maddy asked. "Inviting them to lunch ... the book you gave to the king ... I don't understand what you're up to."

"I told you I'm going to appeal to the king in Lord Hector's way. If it works, I may beat him at his own game. If it doesn't, I may be the second person hung on the gallows this Saturday."

CHAPTER ELEVEN

That evening, Tabby, breathless and red-faced, ran into Annison's chambers just as the clock struck eight. "A servant has just come from the king!" she exclaimed.

Annison, who was trying to decide what to wear for tomorrow's lunch, looked up anxiously. "A servant from the king?" she asked.

"He wants you to come to his Reception Hall immediately. He wants an audience with you."

Annison swallowed hard. "What on earth could he want with me now?"

"The servant didn't say. But you must hurry."

Annison raced to a standing mirror to be sure her dress and hair looked all right. "Do I look presentable?" she asked anxiously.

"There's no time!" Tabby cried impatiently.

"May I come with you?" Maddy asked.

"The king wants her *alone*," Tabby emphasized.

Annison leaned to Maddy's ear. "Watch from the passageway," she whispered.

Annison and Tabby hurried out. Maddy waited for a minute and then, when she was sure it was clear, went to the hidden door in the bedroom, lit the torch, and rushed down the passageway to the peephole.

Maddy got to the peephole before Annison reached the Reception Hall. The king was seated on his throne, flipping through the small, red-velvet book Annison had given him earlier. His expression was one of deep concentration. He looked puzzled and worried, an unusual combination for him. Then a servant entered and announced that Queen Annison had arrived. The king stood up, tucked the book in his belt, and said, "Please send her in."

Queen Annison entered, and, glancing quickly in the direction of the peephole, she bowed. The king went to her and took both her hands in his. "Thank you for coming on such short notice," he greeted.

"The pleasure is mine, sire," she replied.

He kissed her hands and then led her to two of the chairs at the base of the podium on which the throne sat. She sat down in one, and he sat in the other.

"How may I serve Your Majesty?" she asked.

"I want to talk to you about this story you've written." He pulled the book from his belt and held it up.

"What of it, sire?"

"I found it both moving and frustrating at the same time."

"I'm glad my writing could touch your emotions."

"You knew very well that it would. I may not be a particularly brilliant man, but I'm not a fool. You wrote this story for a purpose."

"What purpose might that be, sire?"

"Don't be coy, Annison. I had hoped that you respected me more than that."

"I'm sorry if I sound coy."

"Let's talk about this story." The king fiddled with the pages of the book as he spoke. "You tell about a man who works in a palace and has raised an orphan girl like his own daughter. He works hard and serves his king well, but his greatest reward is to see his foster daughter rise to great heights of power and popularity. But this man never reveals that he's the girl's foster father and carries on in his meager duties. Then one day he learns of a plot to kill the king. He secretly informs the queen, who then tells the king, who then thwarts the plot. But because the king didn't know of this man's loyalty, he believes the slander of those in his court who falsely accuse the man for their own gain—they themselves were in on the plot to kill the king but cleverly disguised the fact. The king has the man locked up, tortured, and then, finally, hung on the gallows."

"That is the story I told, yes."

"The ending leaves me furious, my queen. My sense of injustice at this man's fate makes my blood boil."

"As you are a just king, I thought it might."

"Confound it, Annison, is this story true? Am I the king?"

"Please, Your Majesty," Annison said carefully. "May we continue to speak of the story as only a story, to see what we may learn from it?"

The king snorted unhappily. "You Marutians love your stories, don't you? It's as if you don't know how to speak directly."

"I don't wish to offend you."

"No, no," he said. "We'll do it your way. Let us speak of this man hypothetically."

"Since the story outraged you with its injustice, do you think, then, that the king should free the man?"

"Of course he should." The king suddenly stood up and paced, his hands clasped behind his back. Maddy wondered if it was a habit picked up from Lord Hector by the king or the other way around. "More than freeing him, the king should honor the man! No generosity should be withheld."

Annison breathed a sigh of relief. "I am happy to hear you say so, my lord."

"Now tell me, Annison. Is this story of yours true or not?"

"It is, Your Majesty."

The king groaned. "And who is the man?"

"His name is Simet. He's the one who told me of the plot to poison you, which he'd heard from a reliable source."

"I think I know him. He's one of the palace guards."

"He was, Your Majesty. But even now he is in the dungeons, being tortured."

"I will soon remedy that. And his foster daughter? Have I met her as well?"

Annison opened her mouth to answer, but at that moment a knock came at the door.

"What is it?" the king bellowed.

Lord Hector entered, clutching a handful of papers. "Your Majesty, I have these papers for you to—" He stopped when he saw the queen sitting with the king. "I'm so sorry, sire. I didn't realize you were busy."

He bowed as if to retreat, but the king called him forward. "You are just the man I want to see," the king declared.

"Sire?"

"Yes," the king replied. "There's a grave injustice I want to correct. Will you help me?"

"With pleasure, sire."

Annison suddenly interrupted. "Perhaps Your Majesty should speak *hypothetically* to Lord Hector, to gain his wisdom on the subject," she suggested.

"An excellent idea, my queen," he said boylike, as if he were about to play a game of charades. "Lord Hector, what would you think if I said there was a man who saved a king's life but was not properly rewarded for it?"

Lord Hector looked from the king to the queen and back again before responding, "Then I would assume Your Majesty would want to reward him in some way."

"With great honors, yes?"

"If Your Majesty pleases." Lord Hector's face lit up, and

then he asked, "Do I know this man?"

"I'll say only that he has served me with great diligence in the past month, and I'm afraid I haven't given him his due."

"In the past month?" Lord Hector suddenly blushed.

"Yes," the king went on. "Now, I wonder what *you* would do to honor such a man."

"Well ..." Lord Hector began, again blushing, "I would suggest a banquet, inviting all of his family and friends and the notables of the city, and then I would present him with a medal or medallion of some sort, proclaiming his value to Your Majesty. And"—he paused to clear his throat—"if you felt that this particular servant was worthy, you might give him a house and lands in the countryside. But that is for Your Majesty to decide."

Something about Lord Hector's expression and the way he spoke gave Maddy the impression that he thought he himself was the man about whom the king was talking.

"I'm so glad to hear you say it!" the king exclaimed. "We will do all that for the man—and more."

Lord Hector smiled. "Your Majesty is too kind."

The king frowned. "If I were kind, this man would not be in the dungeon in the first place."

Lord Hector looked puzzled. "In the dungeon?"

"Yes. And it's my intention to find out who put him there in such an unjust manner."

"It ..." Lord Hector suddenly seemed to have trouble speaking. His mouth moved, but the words were slow to come. "It goes without saying. But, sire, who is the man?"

"His name is Simet."

Lord Hector's face contorted as the blood rushed from his face. His expression went from shock to confusion to fear. "Simet?"

"Yes. I assume you know him."

"I do, Your Majesty." Lord Hector struggled to maintain his composure. Maddy was sure his mind was working quickly to turn this to his advantage somehow. "But—oh, dear—this is most awkward."

"Why?"

"*You* authorized his arrest."

Clever man, Maddy thought. *He has turned the tables on the king.*

"Did I?" the king asked, unsure.

"Earlier today. He's the palace guard of whom I told you. He refused to sign the oath of allegiance."

The king looked thoughtful. "Odd, then, that a man who refused to sign your oath is also a man who may have saved my life."

"True, Your Majesty. *If* he did as you said," Hector offered.

"You have your sources of information about this man, and so do I," the king retorted. "For the time being, I will believe *my* sources."

"As you wish, sire. But there's more to it than that. I have reason to believe he's a fanatic of the Old Faith."

"Yes, so you said earlier today."

"Which is one more reason he was put in the dungeon, as *you* authorized."

The king pondered this statement for a moment. "So I authorized his arrest based on *your* claims against him?"

"Yes, sire."

The king looked down at the red-velvet book thoughtfully, then gazed at the queen with a knowing expression. She simply returned his gaze with a look of expectation.

"I think I understand now."

Lord Hector seemed sure he had won his case. "So to

release him from the dungeon might be folly on your part—"

"Folly?" the king bellowed, suddenly turning on Hector. "You speak to your king of his folly?"

"No, Your Majesty. Of course not," Lord Hector said evasively. "I didn't mean *your* folly. I meant—"

"I know what you meant," the king growled. "Regardless, you will release the man. And not only will you release him, but I also want you to begin preparations for the honors you mentioned."

"The honors?" Lord Hector gulped loudly.

"I want him to have a banquet and a medal and a house and lands."

Hector closed his eyes as if enduring great pain. "If you insist, Your Majesty."

"I insist. We will discuss the matter further tomorrow."

"Perhaps we could discuss it at our luncheon together?" Annison suggested.

"That would be perfect," the king agreed. "A woman's touch for such an occasion would be welcome. You are dismissed, Lord Hector."

"Yes, yes," Hector stammered, still dumbfounded by this turn of events. "Thank you, sire."

When Lord Hector reached the door, the king suddenly called out, "Hector, have you been *interrogating* Simet in your usual fashion?"

"*I* haven't as yet. But he has been asked one or two questions, I'm sure."

"Then you had better make sure the palace doctor attends to him. I want him in perfect condition for his banquet."

"Yes, sire." Lord Hector bowed and backed out of the hall.

Once the door was closed, the king turned to Annison again. "Satisfied?" he asked.

"Thank you, sire."

"Well, I'm not," he stated. "You haven't told me everything. I believe there's more to this story than you've said. And I am now suspicious of its outcome."

"There is more," Annison replied. "But it can wait until our luncheon tomorrow."

"Perhaps I won't wait. I have my own ways of finding things out."

Annison smiled at him noncommittally.

The king looked at her warily. "Why do I have the feeling you're toying with me?"

Annison looked offended at the idea. "Your Majesty is far too astute to be *toyed* with."

"Nonsense! People have been toying with me my entire life. From the nursery to the grave, a king is but a toy to be tossed to and fro between his lords and ministers."

"But by his wife?" Annison asked.

"I hope," he said earnestly, "that my wife does not."

He kissed her hands again, and Annison left. Then, alone, he returned to his throne and sat down wearily. His fingers lightly brushed the velvet on Annison's book. He held it to his chest for a moment. Maddy suddenly realized that the king was truly in love with his queen.

He abruptly stood up and went to the door. A servant appeared in the doorway. The king whispered something Maddy couldn't hear. The servant nodded and rushed off, and the king returned to his throne with a wan smile on his face.

CHAPTER TWELVE

⟢ ——————— ⟣

Simet was taken to a wing of the palace Maddy had never seen before. The royal doctor kept an infirmary there, made up of small rooms with comfortable beds. Simet lay in his bed, his face puffed and bruised, but he didn't look as bad as Maddy had feared.

"What has happened?" Simet asked, his voice weak. "Why was I released?"

"Annison spoke to the king," she answered.

His eyes grew wide. "She spoke to him? About what? What did she tell him? Is she in danger?"

"No," Maddy assured him. "She is well, and you are free."

"But what about Lord Hector? His purge is coming in only a few days."

"Annison is doing the best she can to stop it."

"But how?"

"By the inspiration of the Unseen One," Maddy replied, repeating what Annison had told her to say.

"I don't understand," Simet said, sweat forming on his brow. "You have to tell me everything."

"She'll tell you nothing more," a voice said from behind Maddy. It was the doctor. He stood looking like an unmade bed, his white hair sticking out in all directions. Had he been roused from bed to attend Simet? Probably. "This girl is going to leave you now so you can rest. I also want to tend to the results of your *interrogation*." He said the word disdainfully, as if he'd seen too many of the victims of Lord Hector's torturers.

"No, wait," Simet requested.

The doctor intervened and forced Maddy out. She waved quickly from the door and said comfortingly, "Don't worry."

But Maddy herself was still worried. It was one thing to tell a clever story and get Simet released from the dungeon, but it was another to save hundreds if not thousands of believers from Hector's purge. Maddy didn't fully understand Annison's thinking or how she still hoped to influence the king, but she hoped and prayed that Annison would succeed somehow.

As Maddy rounded the corner to the hall leading back to Annison's chambers, Lord Hector stepped forward.

Maddy cried out.

"Calm down!" Lord Hector snapped. "You'll come to no harm."

Maddy continued to walk toward the chamber doors.

"You are the linchpin to all this somehow," he observed, walking alongside her. "But how? Are you influencing the queen? What is your connection to Simet?"

"I'm sorry, but I must return to the queen," Maddy said, picking up her pace.

"What's the connection between the queen and Simet? Why did she intercede for him? *How* did she intercede for him?"

Maddy didn't answer. The chamber doors were in sight now.

Lord Hector suddenly grabbed Maddy's arm just as she reached the doors.

"Ouch!" she cried out, though it didn't hurt much.

"What is the queen up to?" Hector demanded. "Is she for me or against me?"

"Does it matter?" Maddy asked as she grasped the door

handle. "She's only a simpleminded woman. What can she do to you?"

Maddy pushed the door open. The large, bald-headed guard was just inside and approached them menacingly. He relaxed when he saw Maddy but looked suspiciously at Lord Hector's hand on her arm.

Lord Hector let go. "Tell your queen that she should be careful," he warned. "I've been playing this game—and the king—for years."

"Maybe the rules are changing," Maddy retorted and closed the door on him.

Safe inside the chambers, she found herself grabbing for a cup of water. She felt sick to her stomach from the sheer anxiety of everything that had happened. Once she felt calm again, she went into Annison's bedroom to tell her that Simet was all right.

Maddy's dreams that night were fitful. She saw hundreds of people being led to the gallows, their bodies swinging lifeless at the ends of hundreds of ropes. Lord Hector had succeeded with his purge. He had played the "game" better than Annison.

Then she sat at a table with the king and Lord Hector. They were eating lunch. But Annison's chair was vacant.

"Where is she?" Maddy kept asking.

Finally Lord Hector smiled and replied, "She was a fanatic of the Old Faith. You will find her hanging outside."

"No!" Maddy cried.

"What do *you* believe?" the king questioned her. "Are you a fanatic, too, or are you willing to embrace our *new* ideas?"

"What new ideas?" Maddy asked.

"Whatever ideas I approve of," the king responded. He dabbed a napkin against his lips and tossed it carelessly on the table.

"What do you believe?" Lord Hector pressed. "Tell us now so we may decide whether you live or die."

Maddy felt a burning in her eyes. "I believe in the Unseen One," she replied, her voice quivering.

"I'll kill you for that," Lord Hector said with a smile as he tugged on a long rope hanging from the ceiling. A curtain suddenly parted on the far side of the room. Behind it was a small scaffold. A noose hung from the top. "Custom-built for a girl your size," he noted.

"Are you *sure* you believe in the Unseen One?" the king asked with a yawn.

Maddy looked at the scaffold and then back at the king. "Yes," she said as firmly as she could muster. "Yes, I do."

And then she awoke in a cold sweat.

"Whatever happens at lunch tomorrow," she heard herself praying to the Unseen One, "let me be brave."

The morning was filled with preparations for the lunch. A large table was placed in the center of the queen's chambers for Annison, the king, and Lord Hector. Smaller tables were brought in to hold the various dishes of fowl, vegetables, fruits, and several types of bread.

Annison checked and double-checked to make sure everything was as perfect as it could be. Tabby huffed and puffed as she double-checked Annison's double-checking. Maddy ran several errands from the chambers to the kitchen and had to endure the complaints of the royal chef as he upbraided her for interrupting him so much.

Finally the time arrived for the king and Lord Hector to arrive. Annison's entire court stood at strategic places around the table—some to serve, some to make sure the cups were always filled with drinks, others to clear away any unused dishes, and the remainder to do whatever was asked of them. Maddy was assigned to be Annison's special attendant, to stay near Annison in case she needed anything. Maddy was pleased to obey. She had feared she would be sent from the room and not allowed to watch what happened.

"What are you going to do?" Maddy whispered to Annison in the final seconds of silence before the knock came at the door.

"I don't know," Annison answered honestly.

"You mean you don't really have' a plan?" Maddy asked, surprised.

"I have planted some seeds which I hope we will see grow," she replied. "Unless, of course, the birds have plucked them from the ground before they've had a chance."

Maddy wasn't sure of what she meant, but there was no time to question further. A loud rapping sounded on the door. Tabby opened it, and the king and Lord Hector strode in together.

"Oh, my!" the king exclaimed as he looked at the table spread out before him. "I thought we were having a modest lunch. This looks more like a banquet."

"I am undeserving of such a feast," Lord Hector said silkily.

They sat down with Annison, and her staff began to serve them. They chitchatted about the wonderful weather they'd been having and the flowers in the garden, and the queen advised Lord Hector about some of the shops for men in Sarum where he could buy the best-made clothes. He seemed grateful for the advice.

Finally the meal was finished, and the servants brought them coffee, tea, and small chocolates. Both the king and Lord Hector made a fuss about how wonderful the food was and how gracious a hostess Annison had been.

"I do not know Your Highness very well," Lord Hector admitted to her. "But I'm so pleased to find you as charming and delightful as I'd heard you were."

"Thank you," Annison replied.

"You have outdone yourself, my queen," the king said contentedly. "Ask me for anything, anything at all, and it's yours!"

Annison smiled. "I want only what you want, my king— truth and justice in our kingdom."

The king leaned back in his chair and nodded. "Truth and justice, yes. Two things we must have. Shall we begin with truth?" The king then pulled Annison's red-velvet book from his coat pocket and set it down on the table. "Do you read much, Hector?"

Lord Hector looked at it distrustfully. "Occasionally. Books of trade, mostly."

"You should read stories," the king suggested. "Stories can be far more interesting than books of trade. They can also nudge you toward great truths that might otherwise escape you." He patted the book. "This story, for example. Simple as it is, it has caused me to reconsider many things."

"What kinds of things, sire?" Lord Hector inquired.

"That man, for one, the guard who was in the dungeon ..."

"Simet," Annison reminded him.

"Yes, him."

"I released him as you commanded, sire," Lord Hector said quickly.

"I know you did. And I've been informed that he's recovering nicely from your interrogations."

"I did not interrogate him," Lord Hector corrected him.

"No, you didn't. True. Your man Reginald actually did the interrogation."

Lord Hector raised an eyebrow. He clearly didn't expect the king to know about Reginald—or anything to do with what went on in the dungeon. "Reginald?"

"You know him, of course. Suspicious-looking fellow with a rather high forehead."

"Yes, I know him."

"So you should. He does a lot of your dirty work, I understand."

Lord Hector didn't reply but waited to see what the king would say next.

"The same sort of dirty work he did for his previous employer."

"I'm at a loss," Lord Hector said. "I don't know who his previous employer was."

"But you must," the king insisted. "His previous employer was that traitor Lord Terrence."

Lord Hector feigned surprise. "Was he?"

"Yes, he was." The king suddenly patted his pockets as if he'd forgotten something. He then dug into an inside pocket and produced a piece of paper. "Late last night, I got him to tell me all about it."

Lord Hector paused for a moment, then signaled to one of the servants for more water. "You spoke to Reginald yourself?" he asked as innocently as he could.

"At length," the king replied. "You see, I read this story—written by my dear wife—and it caused me to think about the men who had tried to poison me. Of course, I hadn't investigated the case myself. I left it to *you*, my trusted chancellor, to do that. Sadly, everyone who might have been forthcoming with information died from your interrogations."

"I reported that to you at the time," Lord Hector reminded him.

"One of the men was a servant," the king went on. "You accused him of being in the employ of one of the two lords and claimed he had been the one who actually poisoned my cup. But I've learned from Reginald that the accused servant was innocent. It was Reginald who poisoned my cup."

Lord Hector's jaw dropped. "No, my king! Tell me it isn't so!"

"I'm afraid it is. Reginald confessed it all."

"I am stricken!" Hector declared, putting a hand to his mouth. "I had no idea I was employing a *traitor.* Until this moment, I didn't know he was Terrence's man."

"It surprises me what you know and do not know, Lord Hector."

"What do you mean, sire?"

"You said conclusively that Lords Stephen and Terrence were both fanatical members of the Old Faith. I have learned otherwise. In fact, the two of them, along with Reginald, actively *hated* the Old Faith. So how did you draw your conclusions?"

"From my interrogations, sire. But under such duress, they may have lied to me about their cause."

"Perhaps they did." The king drummed his fingers on the book. "Or perhaps you put the lie into their dead mouths."

"Sire!" Hector cried indignantly and stood up.

"Sit down, Hector."

"But Your Majesty—"

Maddy wasn't sure how it happened, but the king suddenly had a knife in his hand. "I said, sit down."

Lord Hector obeyed.

"We were speaking of truth, and now I want it." The king kept the knife steadily pointed at Lord Hector. "You and Lord Stephen and Lord Terrence conspired together to do two things, kill me and—"

"No ! "

"And rid the land of those who subscribe to the Old Faith. You failed at the first, but you've worked very hard at the second."

"You accuse me unfairly!"

"And you continue to lie to me." He turned to Annison and asked, "How did you know I was going to be poisoned at the banquet?"

"Simet told me."

"And how did Simet know?"

Annison hesitated. Maddy knew she was trying to protect her, to keep her out of what might happen.

Maddy stepped forward. "I told him, Your Majesty," she admitted.

"You?"

"I'd be wary of anything this girl has to say, sire," Lord Hector interjected.

"Quiet!" the king commanded. To Maddy he said, "How did *you* know?"

"I overheard Lord Stephen, Lord Terrence, and Lord Hector plotting to poison you the day of the banquet," Maddy reported.

"You're certain it was the three of them?"

"Yes, sire."

"'Don't believe her, Your Majesty!" Hector pleaded, his voice rising. "She is easily influenced and may be confused by what she saw and heard."

The king ignored him and asked Maddy once more, "Are you *certain* Lord Hector was one of the men?"

"I am positive, sire."

Then, catlike, Lord Hector leapt to his feet and raced for the doors. They opened, but the way was blocked by several guards. He stopped, took a few steps in another direction, and then moved in another, but every exit was covered by the king's men. They grabbed him and dragged him back to the table.

The king stood up and slapped him across the face. "I trusted you, Hector, and you have fed me nothing but lies," the king stated.

"What else could I give you?" Lord Hector spat at him, his eyes narrowing with hatred. "The truth is too hard for you to swallow. It gets in the way of your golf games and wigs and stupid parades. The truth in your hands is like giving a diamond to a fool—you would play marbles with it!"

The king observed him silently for a moment, then confessed, "Yes, you're right, Hector, but I'm willing to change. No, I *will* change. But what am I to do with you? Can *you* change?"

Lord Hector, seeing hope for a reprieve, nodded quickly. "Yes, Your Majesty, I can change. Show mercy to me. Please! You will then see such an amendment of life that even my closest family will not recognize me. Mercy!"

The king turned to Annison. "What does my queen say?" he asked.

"It's not for me to decide," Annison answered. "I can only hope you show him the same mercy that he has shown the believers in the Old Faith over the past month."

The king understood and signaled the guards to take Lord Hector away.

"No!" he cried as he was dragged out, kicking and screaming. "No! Please! Have mercy! Noooooo!"

Everyone was shaken by Hector's exit except the king. He sat down again and calmly picked up Hector's uneaten piece of chocolate. Popping it into his mouth, he told Annison, "And now I want the truth from you."

"Sire?"

"Who is Simet?"

"A member of the palace guard," she replied, then added, "and the man who raised me as his daughter."

The king nodded as if he'd already figured it out. "He is also a leader in the Old Faith, a faith that I myself have outlawed."

"Yes, Your Majesty."

The king kept his eyes fixed on Annison. "Then I may assume that you are also a believer in the Old Faith?"

Annison gazed back at the king. "Yes, Your Majesty."

"So, by the law of Hector's decree and the purge he ordered for this coming Saturday, Simet should be executed."

"Lord Hector planned for him to be the first," Annison stated.

"And, by law, you should also be executed."

"Yes, sire." Her gaze never wavered, her eyes staying firm on the king. "In the end, I would not deny my faith—or my foster father."

The king averted his gaze, looking down at the table

thoughtfully. He touched the red-velvet book again. "I would have preferred that you told me the truth in the beginning."

"I was afraid to," Annison confessed. "The man I knew a month ago seemed so fickle and uncaring that I was certain he would have sent me away. And then what would have happened to my people?"

"And now?"

"Now I see a man to be respected. A man I believe loves me. A man I have grown to love."

The king seemed startled by her remark. "Is that true?"

"It is, sire. I would now trust you with my life—and the lives of those I hold most dear."

He sighed. "So be it." He stood up again and seemed taller somehow, rising to a majestic height. "In light of Hector's treason, I will repeal his decree. Further, because Simet, as a believer in the Old Faith, showed his loyalty to me by being instrumental in saving my life, I will repeal any and all laws that oppress or persecute those who believe in the Old Faith. The gallows that Hector constructed will be used on him alone for his treachery."

Annison fell to her knees and, grabbing the king's hand, kissed it. "My king!" she declared.

"Rise, my queen. What I do, I do because I want to be a just king." He then looked down at her tenderly. "And because I want to be a good husband."

Before Annison could respond, he withdrew his hand and marched from the room.

Annison rose to her feet and stood until he was gone, and then she slumped into her chair again. Her face in her hands, she began to cry.

Maddy went to her and wrapped her arms around her neck. She, too, cried.

From the corner, Tabby grabbed a handful of chocolates and said, "I'm going to find another job. This one is too stressful!" And she popped the chocolates into her mouth.

CHAPTER THIRTEEN

The banquet for Simet was held in the Great Hall on the following Saturday. It was a magnificent feast and included all those of the Old Faith whom Lord Hector had thrown into the dungeon. Together they, along with the king and queen, lamented those who had died at Lord Hector's hands. Then the king made a passionate speech asking for their forgiveness and promising a new day of religious freedom for the people of Marus.

Simet, whose bruises were now faded, was touched by the occasion. He was teary-eyed when the king pinned the medal to his chest. "I don't know when I became such a baby," Simet sniffled.

The king laughed and then announced that Simet was now *Lord* Simet, with a manor house and lands to the east of Sarum, and would replace Lord Hector as his adviser.

Annison had the last word, though, when she stood up and, in defiance of all known ceremony and protocol, offered a toast to her *father*, Simet.

Everyone, the king included, rose to his feet and saluted Simet. Afterward, the guests all applauded the queen, for everyone knew by then that she had truly saved their lives.

Alone, in a courtyard on the other side of the palace, Lord Hector was executed for his crimes against the king and against Marus. The executioner and a lone witness confirmed his punishment and signed the death certificate. He was buried in an unmarked grave.

CHAPTER FOURTEEN

———❧—————❧———

"On your next birthday, you'll be old enough to be made a royal lady-in-waiting," Annison told Maddy several days after Simet's banquet. They were in the east garden, walking among the many rows of flowers. The smells were intoxicating.

Maddy smiled. "I don't know what a lady-in-waiting does, but it sounds very chivalrous," she said happily. "Just like something from the days of King Arthur."

"King who?" Annison asked.

Maddy giggled. "I'll tell you about him sometime," she replied.

On the edge of her giggle, though, she had a strange feeling, a sweet sadness. She knew somehow that she would never tell the story to Annison. It was time for her to go home. But she had no idea how or when it would happen.

"You're happy here, aren't you?" Annison asked.

"Yes, I am," she answered. But her tone betrayed her homesickness.

"You miss your family."

Maddy nodded.

"There's a meeting of the Old Faith tonight. I suggest we put it to the leaders to pray that the Unseen One will take you home."

"Can they do that?"

Annison tilted her head a little. "They can *try.*"

The king was on a patch of green grass several yards away. He stood over a small, white ball with a golf club in his hands.

He was practicing his golf swing and had been doing so for the past hour. So far he had succeeded in hitting only one ball in the direction he'd intended.

Now he swung his club backward and then forward, hitting the ball hard. He looked ahead expectantly, hoping to see it fly farther out onto the manicured lawn. Instead, however, it spun off to the side and landed under his royal coach, which had been parked there by the driver.

"Oh, blast!" the king said.

Annison laughed.

He looked at her with a pained expression and informed her with mock sternness, "It isn't funny."

Annison put a hand over her lips to hide the smile, but it lit up her face too much. "I'm sorry," she giggled.

The king then laughed, too. "Maybe I'll take up bowling," he said. He patted his pockets and then added, "I'm out of balls anyway."

"I'll get you one," Maddy shouted and ran to the coach to retrieve the ball he'd just lost. She looked around the wheels for it but couldn't see where it was. Then, stooping down, she saw it sitting under the center of the carriage. Crawling carefully so as not to get her dress dirty, she went to the ball and grabbed it.

"You shouldn't be under there!" she thought Annison called out. But it didn't sound like Annison.

"What?" she asked as she turned to look back. Her mother was peering in at her through the gap in the trellis. Maddy gasped, rising up and nearly hitting her head on the underside of the porch.

"Come out of there!" her mother ordered. "You'll get your dress all dirty."

Maddy crawled out from under the porch.

Her mother *tsked* at her and brushed at her dress. "Why do we make you new dresses when you insist on getting them dirty?" she asked. "Why?"

Johnny Ziegler suddenly rushed up to her. "There you are! I found you!" he screeched happily, touching her as if to ensure that it was her turn to find him.

Maddy blinked. "You won't believe what just happened to me," she told her mother.

Her mother sighed as the baby cried from the other side of the lawn. "You're right," she said as she walked away. "I probably won't."

"What's that?" Johnny pointed at her hand.

"What's what?" Maddy asked. She felt a little fuzzy-headed.

Johnny pointed again.

Maddy lifted her hand. She was clutching something she'd found under the porch.

It was a golf ball.

EPILOGUE

As usual, Whit and Jack had dozens of questions to ask when they finished the manuscript. But there was no one to ask except for Mrs. Walston.

"She won't tell us anything, you know," Jack said as they walked up to her front porch.

"It won't hurt to try," Whit replied as he knocked on the door.

Mrs. Walston opened the inside door. She didn't seem surprised to see them. Whit opened the storm door to hand her the manuscript.

He opened his mouth to speak, but the look on her face blocked any hope for answers. If she knew anything at all, she wasn't going to reveal it to them.

Maybe some other time. On another day.

"Thank you for returning it to me," she offered as she clutched the school notebook to her breast.

Whit managed a smile and said, "Thank you for letting us read it."

"This is for you," she said and produced a small envelope from the pocket of her cardigan. She gave it to him. "It's awfully cold. You should probably read it in the warmth of your car."

The two men took the hint. "Right," Jack agreed, then added under his breath as they walked away, "She's as subtle as a brick."

In the car, Whit looked at the front of the envelope. It was written in a familiar style. It read, "John Avery Whittaker & Jack Allen."

Whit opened the envelope carefully. A single sheet of small notepaper was inside. He unfolded it and read it aloud.

> "I was told that you would like to meet
> me. I'd like to meet with you, too. I'll be in
> touch soon.
>> With regards,
>> James Curtis"

"James Curtis," Jack asked. "Who is James Curtis?"

Whit held up the note and examined it closely, then held it out to Jack. "Do you see, Jack? Look at the handwriting."

Jack's eyes grew wide, and he suddenly pulled out one of the school notebooks and flipped it open. "I see," he said excitedly. "I see."

There was no mistaking it. Sure, it was older and a little more jagged, but it was virtually the same. The handwriting on the note was the same as the handwriting in the manuscripts.

Whoever James Curtis was now, he was definitely the one who had chronicled the stories.

Jack put his car into gear. Whit glanced back at the Walston house. Mrs. Walston stood at the door, still clutching the school notebook. She looked sad, Whit thought, as if a cherished secret was now lost forever.

Back at his antique shop, Jack read a note from his wife explaining that she was out looking over some antiques in Connellsville. Several clocks ticked around him—all of them from different periods of the eighteenth, nineteenth, and twentieth centuries. They all reminded him that it was lunch-time, but he was too distracted for food.

Sitting down at his desk, he opened his briefcase and took out a file he had started on the Marus stories. Inside were his notes about Kyle and Anna, Wade, and Maddy. He wanted to write down a few thoughts about this new story and the "clues" it contained.

"Maddy," he wrote. Then he amended it to read, "Maddy Nichols." Then underneath that he added, "Madina Nicholaivitch."

It was another name to cross-reference at the library and the records in City Hall.

Looking at the name once again, he suddenly remembered something. He rifled through the pages of the file until he found a photocopy of an article he'd picked up at the library. It was Maude McCutcheon's obituary. But unlike many obituaries, this was an extended report about her life—in appreciation for her many years of teaching in Odyssey.

He picked up the phone and dialed Whit's office number. On the second ring, Whit picked up. "Hello?"

"I'm looking at Maude McCutcheon's obituary," Jack said.

"And?"

"It says here that Maude became Maude *McCutcheon* after she married Richard McCutcheon of Connellsville."

Whit seemed to know there was more. "Go on."

"Her maiden name was Nichols."

The line hissed as Whit paused again. "No kidding," he finally said.

Jack went on, "According to this, her classmates in the teacher's college called her *Maude* because they thought her nickname was too childish and her real name too weird."

Whit knew the answer to his question, but he asked anyway, just to hear Jack say it. "So her given name was ... "

"Madina."

"Maybe I should have a look at that article," Whit said.

Jack smiled. "Maybe you should."

And now, a preview of the exciting Passages, Book 4!

PROLOGUE

Whit's End stood waiting like an old friend. The porch stretched across the front of the Victorian-style building like a broad smile. The windows, like eyes, flashed in the winter sunlight. The melting snow hung from its head like a white beret.

John Avery Whittaker, or Whit as he was better known, mounted the steps to the front door. The winter wind gently blew his wild, white hair around his forehead. Jack Allen, his good friend, followed behind him with his head tilted down and his hands buried deep in his coat pockets. They'd just had lunch together and now returned to Whit's End so Whit could check on things.

The bell above the door jingled as they entered. It was early afternoon, so the booths and tables of the section of Whit's End that served as a soda fountain were filled with kids chatting, eating, finishing their homework, or doing all three at the same time. A hum of noise came from other parts of the building as well: the toy train whistle from the "county's largest train set"; a rehearsal of a play going on in the Little Theater; The Imagination Station at work upstairs; and the general noises from the many other rooms filled with kids, gadgets, and gizmos Whit had created to make Whit's End a fascinating place for kids to play and learn.

Connie Kendall, a teen who served as one of Whit's employees, stood behind the counter dishing out ice cream to one of the regulars.

"Hi, Whit, Jack," she called out pleasantly. She brushed a lock of her dark hair away from her slender, attractive face and up under her paper work hat.

"Hello, Connie," the two men said. Jack sat down on a stool at the counter, while Whit took off his coat to hang on a hook near the kitchen door.

"Where've you been all day?" she asked. Connie was naturally curious and loved to know what kinds of things Whit got into when he wasn't at the shop.

"Didn't you get my note?" Whit asked.

"No," she replied.

Whit's hand instinctively went to his coat pocket, where his fingers lightly touched the edge of an envelope. He'd forgotten to leave the note for her. "Oh," he said. An embarrassed smile formed on his lips but was hidden by his thick, white mustache. "I never got around to dropping it off for you."

"What did the note say?" Connie asked.

"Only that Jack and I were running errands."

"Errands?"

Jack swiveled off the stool. "Did you tell her about the

manuscripts, Whit?" he asked as he went around the counter to pour himself a cup of coffee.

"I mentioned them in the note."

"Which I didn't get," Connie jabbed at him. "What manuscripts?"

Jack explained, "A few days ago I found an old school notebook in the bottom of a trunk formally owned by Maude McCutcheon."

"I remember Mrs. McCutcheon. She taught English literature, right?"

"Among other things," Whit affirmed.

"Anyway," Jack continued, "the notebook had a hand-written story in it that took place back in the 1950s. It was about a brother and a sister from Odyssey who somehow traveled to an alternate world—an alternate dimension, I guess you could say—to a land called Marus."

"Marus? I've never heard of it."

"Neither had we," Whit said.

"I guess it was a really good story if the two of you were so interested in it," Connie observed.

"Actually, it was the first of *three* stories that we've been able to find," Whit clarified. "The first was in the trunk, the second was in Maude McCutcheon's study, and the third was being kept by Mrs. Walston, the mother of a boy named Wade who had slipped into Marus in 1945."

Connie held up her hand. "Wait a minute! You're talking about these people as if they're real."

"That's the strange thing, Connie. The people in the stories *are* real," said Whit. "We haven't been able to find the brother and sister from the first story, but the boy from the second story actually *lived* here in Odyssey."

"Really? Have you talked to him?"

"He died in Vietnam," Jack said sadly

"Oh."

"And the *third* story was about Maude McCutcheon herself. She went to Marus back in the '20s."

Connie eyed the two men warily. "Let me get this straight. Are you saying you think these stories are true?"

Whit and Jack looked away without replying.

Connie giggled. "Come on, you guys. Just because some-one wrote stories about real people from Odyssey who traveled to another dimension, that doesn't mean they really happened. Right?" She looked from Whit to Jack and back again. "Right?"

Whit shrugged. "I don't know."

Connie shook her head. "Mrs. McCutcheon probably wrote the stories herself or had her students write them as class assignments."

Jack sipped his coffee. "That's what *we* thought at first."

"Except that Mrs. McCutcheon didn't write them," Whit explained. "Someone called James Curtis did."

"We *think*," Jack corrected him.

"The handwriting in the notebooks and on his note to us are the same." Whit pulled a note from his pocket as evidence. "Whoever this man is, he's still living here in Odyssey somewhere, and he wants to meet us."

"Okay," Connie said, her tone full of disbelief. "So James Curtis has an amazing imagination, and for years and years he's been writing interesting stories about a make-believe place called Marus. It doesn't seem like such a big mystery to me. In fact, it sounds like you two are making it into a bigger mystery than it really is." She smiled at them. "Too much time on your hands, maybe?"

"Maybe," Whit conceded, smiling back at her.

Jack chuckled softly but didn't say anything.

"And maybe," Whit countered, "it's the *possibility* that the stories might be true that has me fascinated. I've spent my life pondering imponderables, asking the question *What if?* That's how I invented The Imagination Station. I asked myself, *what if* we could travel to other times and places to see what happened there? Whit's End happened because I asked, *what if* there was a place in Odyssey where kids could learn and have fun at the same time? Well... *what if* there is another world out there somewhere, in another dimension, and some kids from *our* world could get to it at various times for various reasons? Even if the stories *aren't* true, it's worthwhile to think about the possibilities."

"What do you think, Jack?" Connie asked.

Jack looked thoughtful for a moment, then affirmed, "I agree with Whit. I mean, I'm not convinced the stories are true, but it's been a lot of fun investigating them."

"I'm sure we'll know a lot more when we finally get to meet James Curtis," Whit concluded.

The bell above the door jingled again as a man in a blue uniform stepped in. It was Frank, their mailman. He'd always reminded Connie of the Scarecrow from *The Wizard of Oz* movie. "Special delivery," he said jovially He dropped a large manila envelope on the counter.

"Thanks, Frank," Whit said and picked up the envelope.

Frank waved good-bye and was out the door again before they could say any more.

Whit picked up the envelope. It was addressed to him in a handwriting he'd come to know quite well over the past few days.

"James Curtis?" Jack asked after glancing at the script.

"Looks like it," Whit agreed as he tore open the flap.

"James Curtis sent you a package?" Connie said, then grunted. "If you ask me, he's probably some guy who's been desperate to get his manuscripts published and figured you'd be just the sucker to do it for him."

Whit smiled noncommittally at her. He pulled the contents from the envelope. It was a black school notebook with a white square in the center of the front and black tape on the binding.

"Another story," Jack said with obvious excitement. Connie thought his face, normally calm and passive, seemed to light up just a little. His blue eyes flickered and his cheeks flushed with anticipation.

Whit nodded and flipped open the cover. It was the same handwriting as the others.

"There's a note," Connie observed and pointed to a slip of paper that had fallen onto the counter.

Whit picked it up and read aloud: "Please read—and then bring everything back to me at 10:00 o'clock tomorrow morning, Hillingdale Haven."

"Hillingdale Haven?" Jack asked.

Whit's heart sank a little.

"But isn't that the mental institution outside of town?" Connie inquired.

"I'm afraid it is," Whit replied. His eye scanned the first page of the notebook. It was dated *March 21,1934*. Under that was written: "The Chronicles of the Betrayed."

CHAPTER ONE

James waited in the bushes until the black-and-white police car passed by. The two uniformed men inside turned their heads to and fro as they drove. They were looking for him.

He waited, crouched like a small animal hiding from a predator. When he was sure the road was clear, he grabbed his bundle of goods—bread, cheese, and a slice of apple pie—and stood up. He adjusted the suspenders that were buttoned to his tattered wool trousers. His shirt, once white, was smudged with dirt and grass stains.

His Aunt Edna would scream if she saw the state he was in! She'd make him wash his face and comb his short, brown hair, which now stuck out like a porcupine's quills. But Aunt Edna was probably screaming anyway, he figured. Why else were the police looking for him? This was the third time he'd run away from her in as many weeks.

He gave his cap a tug and sprinted across the black tar to the field on the other side. The weeds were tall, almost like wheat, and would give him easy cover if someone came. He looked ahead to the forest that would provide his way of escape. It was about 100 yards away, across the sea of weeds that moved like waves beneath the gentle breeze.

It was a beautiful spring day, perfect for escaping Aunt Edna.

He was determined not to get caught this time. He had no intention of going back to Aunt Edna and her strict ways. She was a cruel ogre as far as he was concerned, and no law or lectures could persuade him otherwise. When his parents were still alive, they never made him wear the awful clothes she made him wear. Or forced him to read all those books. Or made him do sums and fractions. Or dragged him to church every Sunday morning and Wednesday evening. His parents let him do what he wanted. That's how he liked it.

"You don't understand what it's like," he had said to her during their last argument.

"But I *do*, child," she replied.

But how could she understand what it was like to have your parents lose all their money and their home in this thing called the Great Depression? How did she know what it was like to be left behind with *her* while they packed his two sisters off to nicer relatives around the country? What made her think she knew how it felt when the news came that they'd been killed in a bus crash on their way to California? Killed while going to find work; while going to find a new home; while going to find *life*.

"You don't know! You *can't!*" James had shouted at her, slamming the door to his bedroom as a punctuation mark.

Later, when she had gone out to shop, he had collected his belongings: a torn photo of his family that he shoved into his trouser pocket and his father's ring—given to him after the accident, of course—which he tied on a string and put around his neck. After wrapping up the food in a rag in case he got hungry later, he had slipped out the back door, crept down the alley to avoid the tattletale eyes of the neighbors, and dashed away from the musty, old houses.

James wasn't sure where he'd go. Maybe he could find his two sisters, and then they could all escape together. Maybe they could start a new life in California as their parents had wanted. Maybe—

A horse's whinny caught James's attention. He looked in

the direction of the sound—over there near the woods—and was surprised to see not only one horse but two, and a couple of wagons, at the edge of the trees. The wagons were large and enclosed, like coaches on a train or small houses on wheels, with doors at the back and windows on the sides that were shuttered. James had seen similar wagons when his parents took him to the circus a few years before.

Hope rose in his chest. Maybe a circus had come to a town nearby. Maybe he could join it and become a world-famous trapeze artist and tame lions and get fired out of cannons and travel all over the country!

As if to affirm his hope, a man dressed in an odd costume rounded one of the wagons. He wore a shirt with a rainbow of colors going up and down both sides of it, and he had knee breeches and long, white stockings and black boots. He walked up to a large campfire and began to kick dirt on it, as if to put out the flames.

Funny, James thought, *the horses, the wagons, and the campfire all look like they've been here a while. But I didn't notice any of them when I started across the field. How did I miss them—or that mist that's moved toward me from the forest?*

It was strange to have mist like that in the middle of a sunny spring day. Yet somehow the mist didn't mute the colors of the scene. The green grass, the rainbow colors of the man's shirt, and the remains of the fire were all so vibrant, as if they'd been hand-painted on glass, like stained-glass windows in a church.

It had gotten noticeably cooler in the past few minutes, though, and James's skin went goose-pimply (from the cool air or the feeling that something strange was happening—he didn't know which).

The weirdly dressed man spotted James and stood watching him with his hands on his hips. James wondered if he should run in another direction, just in case the man was the type to take him back to Aunt Edna. But the man was so unlike anyone James had seen in Odyssey that he wanted to believe he'd be friendly, if not sympathetic. The man might even give him a ride somewhere in his wagons. James started walking toward him.

"Hello," James said when he was close enough to the man to be heard.

"Hail," the man replied in a deep, resonant voice. He was a dark-skinned fellow with black hair, thin, black mustache, and a gold earring in his left ear. His eyes were bright and piercing. He looked like Douglas Fairbanks in a motion picture of Zorro that James had seen with his father at a cinema—or like a picture of a gypsy James had once seen. This last thought made him a little nervous. He'd heard that caravans of gypsies wandered the countryside, scavenging food and causing trouble because of the Depression. "What brings you to us?" the man asked.

"I was walking across the field and saw you," James said, then abruptly added, "Are you a gypsy?"

"Gypsy?" the man asked.

"Or part of a circus?"

The man looked perplexed, as if James had used words that made no sense. He said, "We are traders. Are you here on an errand? Perhaps you are a message boy for someone who wishes to do business with us?"

James didn't understand what the man was saying either. "No. I'm by myself," he replied.

"Pity."

"Are you going to Odyssey?"

A puzzled expression spread across the man's face. "Odyssey?"

"The town near here."

The man shrugged indifferently. "We are going up the mountain, if that is what you mean."

"Mountain? What mountain?"

The man gestured toward the mist-covered woods.

James was truly confused now. No mountain stood behind those woods. Any mountains the man expected to find were in the other direction.

Suddenly a young woman came around from the back of the wagon. "We are ready, Papa," she said, then saw James. "Oh."

James was taken aback by her appearance. She had wild, dark hair barely contained by a red scarf. She wore a torn peasant dress that hung loosely from her shoulders. But her eyes really caught his attention: dark and piercing, just like her father's. James thought she may have been the prettiest woman he'd ever seen.

"Who is this?" she asked the man.

"Some boy," he said and began to kick dirt at the fire again. "I want to make sure this fire is out. It wouldn't do to be blamed for burning down the mountain. Connam would have us imprisoned."

"Or one of his sons would execute us."

"All the same."

The young woman turned her attention to James. "Why do you linger, boy?" she asked. "What do you want?"

James was going to say he didn't want anything. He was tempted to walk away from these strange people. But he changed his mind when he suddenly heard car tires screeching to a halt behind him. He spun around and felt his heart jump into his throat as he saw, through the mist, a police car on the road. Two officers climbed out and pointed in his direction. One called out to him.

"Oh, no," James gasped.

"What is the matter with you?" the young woman asked, craning her neck to see what he was looking at.

"The police. I can't let them catch me," James cried as he tried to think of what to do. The woods. They were his best hiding place, he thought.

The young woman looked at James. "The po-*what?*"

"The police! I ran away from my Aunt Edna, and they'll take me back." James watched as the two officers stepped into the field and made their way quickly toward him. "See?"

The young woman looked at James, then followed his gaze across the field. "I see nothing but a field in the sunshine."

"Sunshine! What about the mist?" James exclaimed. It engulfed him now, so that the police came in and out of view. One second he could see their badges flickering in the waning light, their batons swinging from their belts against their legs. The next second, they were lost in a gray curtain. "I have to hide," he said, then ran toward the woods. Ducking behind the largest tree he could find, he waited. He hoped they hadn't seen where he went.

James heard the young woman say in a pleading voice, "Papa!"

"No," the man said, stamping out the last of the fire. "We don't have time for children who are not right in the head."

"Papa, please."

"He's not one of your stray puppies."

"You heard him. He needs our help."

"From what? He talks about mist when it is clear and sunny. He uses words that make no sense. *Po-leese.* What does it mean?"

James ventured a peek around the tree. The officers still hadn't arrived. Maybe they were lost in the mist.

"Papa, *please?*" the young woman said softly.

"Fantya, you are too quick with your sympathy! You would help every stranger who asks for it, and then where would we be?"

"No worse off than we are now," she replied. "Or maybe we are better for it."

The man sighed. "We can take him as far as Dremat," he offered, sounding like a man who had lost this argument many times before. "He could run away from there, if that's what he wants. Does that satisfy you?"

"Yes, Papa. Thank you." Fantya turned and approached James at the tree. "Boy?"

"Go away," James said in a harsh whisper as he ducked behind the tree again. "I don't want them to know where I am."

Fantya waved a hand toward the field. "There is no one there."

"They're in the mist."

"There is no mist," she said firmly. "Look."

James cautiously peered around the tree again. His mouth fell open in astonishment.

The mist was gone.

The police—and their car—had vanished.

CHAPTER TWO

James stared at the open field, bright golden in the sunlight. He was struck by the way all the colors suddenly seemed much more vivid than he'd ever seen before—the blue of the sky a much deeper blue, the green of the trees a far more intense green, and the yellow of the weeds almost shining. But the police were nowhere to be found. "What happened to them?" he asked as he stepped from behind the tree to look more closely.

"You must be hungry, perhaps feverish," the young woman said. "Come into the wagon and I will find you a portion of something to eat."

"A *small* portion to eat!" the man shouted.

"But they were there," James protested. "Their car was on the road and—" James stopped suddenly. The road, which he could see from the field only a moment ago, had also disappeared. "What happened to the road?" he cried out.

Fantya and her father watched curiously as James ran across the field. Finally he stopped and gestured wildly to the ground, shouting back to them, "It was here! I just ran across it! Where did it go?" He paced back and forth, looking down at the ground like someone who'd lost a valuable coin.

"If we leave now, he may not be able to catch up with us," the man said.

Fantya gave him a disapproving look. "Now, Papa," she said, "he is obviously in distress. Look at the poor boy."

The man grunted and began to hitch the horses to the wagons.

✦————————✦

James was grateful to Fantya and her father, who was called Visyn, for the food they gave him and the ride they offered to the nearest town. His confusion was compounded, though, when they told him repeatedly that the nearest town wasn't Connellsville, as he thought, but a large trading town called Dremat.

"What happened to Connellsville?" he asked as Visyn snapped the reins and the horse lurched forward.

"The same thing that happened to your mystery road," Visyn grumbled. "*Poof.* Vanished."

They set off on a rocky road leading up a mountain, for there really was a mountain. And try as he might, James couldn't figure out where the mountain had come from—any more than he could figure out how the road had disappeared.

The other wagon was driven by a man called Nosz who had a thick, dark beard. Visyn's friend and business partner, Nosz was large and barrel-chested and wore clothes like Visyn's, except that he also wore a vest with bangles dangling from the seams that jingled when he moved. Fantya sat next to Nosz on the front bench of his wagon. James couldn't help but glance back at her from time to time, and when he did, he noticed by the way Nosz spoke and acted toward Fantya that he liked her a lot. She didn't seem interested in him, however, which made Nosz pout and complain like a little child who couldn't have what he wanted.

"Why do I waste my time with you?" James heard Nosz say to her once when they stopped to tend to the horses a few hours later.

"I never asked you to waste your time," Fantya replied. "You are welcome to leave whenever you want."

"Maybe I will," Nosz said darkly. "Then where will your father be? He is only half the tradesman I am."

"But you are twice the fool he is!" she snapped. "Where will *you* be without my father's wisdom?"

Nosz growled and stormed off into the gathering sunset.

Fantya turned to James and wiggled a finger at him. "Come with me," she said. "There is someone you haven't met." She led James around to the back of the lead wagon and opened the door. "Go in," she ordered.

James climbed the small steps and went through the door into the dark interior. When his eyes had adjusted to the dimness a minute later, he saw that the inside of the wagon was decorated like a small sitting room. There was a cushioned chair and a small end table with a lacy covering and an oil lamp on top. He noticed a large, open trunk with clothes and blankets inside. A wash table sat under a shuttered window. A long, comfortable-looking sofa stretched along the front. In the corner sat a potbellied stove, its flue pipe jutting up and disappearing through the roof. The walls were a deep brown, and the floor had a worn carpet that might have been red once but had now faded.

What really caught James's attention, however, was a large cot covered in huge pillows and ornately colored blankets. A woman—an older version of Fantya—rested on the cot, smiling gently at him. James took off his cap and held it tightly to his chest.

"This is your stray boy?" the woman asked Fantya.

"His name is James."

The woman waved James forward. "Come into the light. Let me see you."

James moved closer to the cot. The light from a lamp next to the cot splashed white and orange onto the woman's smooth face. *It looks like a mask,* James thought, *framed by her dark hair.* She looked frail, but her eyes were sharp and clear.

"She is Deydra, my mother," Fantya said.

"A pleasure to meet you." James bowed his head politely.

The woman gazed at him from head to foot. "Your clothes are unusual," she observed. "I have never seen such long breeches. Or short boots. Or straps." She waved a bejeweled finger at his chest.

"They're my suspenders."

"Come closer," she said. "Let me see your face."

James obliged her.

Gazing at him, the woman's face suddenly lit up with surprise. "Your eyes!" she said.

James was concerned. "What's wrong with them?" he asked.

"They are two colors, blue and green."

"My eyes are brown," James insisted.

"Are you saying I cannot see? One is blue and the other is green," Deydra maintained. She reached behind her to the end table and picked up a gold-handled mirror. She held it up so James could see his reflection.

James looked closely There was his slender face, the freckles that dotted his nose, and his eyes. He gasped. It was true! One eye was green and the other was blue.

"But ... how did this happen?" he asked. "Honest, lady, I looked in the mirror at my Aunt Edna's this morning, and my eyes were still brown. Like shoe polish, my dad used to say. I would've seen if they'd changed colors."

"Sit down," Deydra said.

Fantya brought a chair forward for him. He sat down slowly, still clutching the mirror and staring at his eyes.

Deydra leaned back against her propped-up pillows. "I have

heard legends of strangers with eyes like yours or strange-colored hair. I have scarcely believed them. Why should I? I have never in my life seen such things. They were legends, that's all—stories people told around campfires to scare one another."

James was speechless. He barely heard what the woman was saying. His eyes. How had they changed colors?

"You've never told me about those legends," Fantya said, disappointed.

"They are not *our* legends," Deydra said. "We Palatians don't believe in the stories of Marus. But I have heard them in our dealings with this country. Now and again someone will whisper of the Unseen One and of His messengers. People with strange-colored eyes that do His bidding. And they say it was a boy with strange-colored hair who brought the illness that destroyed the world hundreds of years ago."

"Are you a messenger for the gods?" Fantya asked James directly.

"The gods?"

Deydra corrected Fantya: "Not *gods*, silly girl. The *Unseen One*."

James was bewildered. "I don't know what you're talking about."

Deydra studied him for a moment. "Tell me where you are from."

James obeyed. For some time, he told Deydra about his father and mother and how he'd been sent to stay with his Aunt Edna in Odyssey and how much he disliked her and how he kept running away to find his two sisters and take them somewhere so they could start over again as a family.

Deydra listened earnestly, then probed him with questions about his "homeland." Over the next hour, James found himself trying to explain things like cars and policemen and electricity and planes. He was soon so busy talking that he didn't notice when Fantya slipped out of the wagon, and he barely noticed the jolt and rocking of the wagon as they continued their journey up the mountain.

When Deydra had run out of questions and James felt parched from talking so long, they each had a cup of something cool that tasted spicy but refreshing. Then the woman spoke thoughtfully. "You are either a clever liar, a very gifted storyteller, or from another world," she said. "Which is it?"

"I'm not lying," James said.

"Then you have been telling me stories?"

"No," he said firmly. "I'm not making it up."

"Then ..." she hesitated, giving James enough time to draw his own conclusion.

James suddenly laughed. "I'm not from another world," he said. "I *can't* be."

"What you have described sounds nothing like *this* world, I can assure you."

James couldn't decide what to do. The woman didn't seem insane. But what was he supposed to think when she talked about other worlds?

"If I'm from another world, then where am I now?" he asked.

"At the moment, you are in the land of Marus."

"Never heard of it."

"But you're here."

"I don't believe it."

Deydra quickly reached over and pinched James's arm. He jerked backward and cried out, "Hey, what's the big idea? What was that for?"

"To make sure you aren't dreaming."

A small, red welt formed where she had pinched him.

"This is nuts," he said as he rubbed his arm. "How could I go to another world? I'm not Flash Gordon. I didn't get in one of those rocket ships to the moon. I was running across the field."

"Fantya told me you saw a mist that no one else saw."

"Yeah, so?"

"Perhaps it was an enchanted mist. A mist that carried you to this land."

"I don't believe it," James said adamantly, his jaw set.

Deydra spoke angrily, waving a hand as if to dismiss him. "Then go away," she said. "If you do not believe, why should I? What is to stop me from deciding that you are out of your mind or delirious with a fever that has changed the color of your eyes? By rights, I should throw you from this wagon and let you make your own way. Or better still, I could turn you in to the authorities at Dremat. They have places for people who have gone insane."

"But I'm not insane!"

"Then stop arguing with me and listen," she said, then softened her tone. "You are here. This much we can't deny. By your own confession, you do not know anything about this land. Sit and keep your mouth closed and I will tell you the way of things."

James noticed then that he'd wrung his cap like a wet dishrag.

"Unlike my own country of Palatia, Marus is not ruled by a king but is a collection of fiefdoms," the woman began. "Some families who emerged from the ashes of the previous world, the world that existed before the Great Catastrophe, have secured and maintained their positions of power. Some have become slaves. Some even disappeared completely. The powerful families rule what can be ruled of Marus. They nego- tiate the peace with one another and conduct business with the neighboring countries. This is why we travel from Palatia to the southern part of Marus. We trade with the family that owns the land, this mountain, the forests, and the mines of the south: the family of Connam."

The woman talked on and on. And James, feeling as if he were listening to Aunt Edna again, struggled hard to concentrate. But his mind kept returning to one thought: *How am I going to get out of here?*

Eventually he asked permission to let some air into the musty, old wagon. He opened the shutter on one of the windows, and the cool smell of pine blew in. He breathed deeply.

Standing at the window, James looked at Deydra and wondered how someone so sweet could be so completely mad. To think that he'd somehow stumbled from one world to another was ... well ... more than he was willing to believe. He didn't care what she said about Marus or who was in charge or legends about Unseen Ones or whatever else she made up. It wasn't possible.

He wondered what would happen if he suddenly made a break for the door and ran off. Would they come after him? Probably not. What was he to them? Just a runaway boy. That's all he was to anyone.

So why not run for it *now*?

James checked the path to the door. Nothing stood in his way. The frail woman couldn't grab for him. His muscles tensed throughout his body. He could do it. He *should* do it. What was the use of staying here with these people?

He glanced out the window. If they were on a mountain, it would be foolish to leap out the door and roll off a cliff. He saw the dirt road and thick trees off to the side. His eyes wandered through the branches to the terrain beyond. It was dark now and hard to see, making him realize they had talked away the day, but he could still make out the upward slope. Suddenly, the wagon passed a clearing in the trees, and James saw a valley in the distance below. He thought he could make out the flickering lights of a town. Then he became aware of a great light that shone pale across the entire scene. His eyes turned up to the night sky, and instantly he felt as if someone had struck him in the chest with a sledgehammer.

"No!" he whispered.

"What's wrong, boy?" Deydra asked.

James couldn't speak. Even if he could've, he wouldn't have known the words to say. But in that moment, he realized the woman wasn't out of her mind after all. Neither was he, for his own eyes couldn't deny what he was seeing at that very moment.

There, high above him, was a sky with *two moons*. One was large and white, and the other was about half the size and slightly more orange.

FOCUS ON THE FAMILY®

At Focus on the Family, we work to help you really get to know Jesus and equip you to change your world for Him.

We realize the struggles you face are different from your parents' or your little brother's, so we've developed a lot of resources specifically to help you live boldly for Christ, no matter what's happening in your life.

Besides exciting novels, we have Web sites, magazines, booklets, and devotionals . . . all dealing with the stuff you care about.

Breakaway
Teen guys
breakawaymag.com

Brio
Teen girls
briomag.com

Focus on the Family Magazines

We know you want to stay up-to-date on the latest in your world — but it's hard to find information on entertainment, trends, and relevant issues that doesn't drag you down. It's even harder to find magazines that deliver what you want and need from a Christ-honoring perspective.

That's why we created *Breakaway* (for teen guys), *Brio* (for teen girls), and *Clubhouse* (for tweens, ages 8 to 12). So, don't be left out — sign up today!

Clubhouse
Tweens ages 8 to 12
clubhousemagazine.com

Adventures in
ODYSSEY®
Weekly Radio Show
whitsend.org

Phone toll free: (800) A-FAMILY (232-6459)

Their town is Ambrosia . . . their headquarters is a vintage B-17 bomber . . . and they are The Last Chance Detectives . . . four ordinary kids who team up to solve mysteries no one else can be bothered with. Now, for the first time, the three best-selling episodes in the series are available in one DVD gift set.

Request this collector's edition set by calling the number below. And see if you can crack the cases of *Mystery Lights of Navajo Mesa*, *Legend of the Desert Bigfoot*, and *Escape from Fire Lake*.

And for the latest audio exploits of The Last Chance Detectives, call that same number. Request your copy of *The Day Ambrosia Stood Still*, *Mystery of the Lost Voices*, and *Last Flight of the Dragon Lady*.